WILD PORK AND WATER- CRESS

THE NOVEL BEHIND THE FEATURE FILM
HUNT FOR THE WILDERPEOPLE

BARRY CRUMP

PENGUIN BOOKS

PENGUIN

UK | USA | Canada | Ireland | Australia
India | New Zealand | South Africa | China

Penguin is an imprint of the Penguin Random House group
of companies, whose addresses can be found at
global.penguinrandomhouse.com.

Penguin
Random House
New Zealand

First published by Barry Crump Associates, 1986
This edition published by Penguin Random House New Zealand, 2016

Cover and text design by Carla Sy © Penguin Random House New Zealand
Cover photograph and *Hunt for the Wilderpeople* stills by Kane Skennar
© Majestical Pictures Limited, 2015
Image on page 7: Barry Crump with his dogs. Photograph taken by
Mark Coote. Further negatives of the *Evening Post* newspaper.
Ref: EP/1992/0513/19A-F. Alexander Turnbull Library, Wellington,
New Zealand. http://natlib.govt.nz/records/22496098
Colour separation by Image Centre Group
Printed and bound in Australia by Griffin Press,
an Accredited ISO AS/NZS 14001 Environmental
Management Systems Printer

A catalogue record for this book is available from the
National Library of New Zealand.

ISBN 978-0-14-357374-6
eISBN 978-1-74-348714-3

penguinrandomhouse.co.nz

FSC
www.fsc.org
MIX
Paper from
responsible sources
FSC® C009448

CONTENTS

2 9 AUG 2023

DEAR
≈ **READER** ≈

I never lived with my father, but we did catch up several times before he passed away on 3 July 1996, aged sixty-one. One of our catch-ups lasted a year. I was very thankful for that, as we forged a friendship that never left us. The time I'd like to share with you, though, was in the mid-1980s.

We'd arranged to meet on mutual ground at my brother's place in Putaruru. Barry had arrived before me, and I was surprised his sidekick this time was not a woman but a nine-year-old Maori boy called Coonch. They were very relaxed and comfortable with each other, which is more than I can say for the old man and me; we were meeting for the first time in years.

Next morning we drove for several hours to Barry's place in Opotiki. It wasn't legal or ethical, but the nine-year-old drove while Barry sat in the passenger seat, telling the rest of us that it was more nerve-racking for him than it was for his young driver, Coonch. There was one brief stop, just before we reached Barry's, when Coonch ordered the dog up a bank next to the road. A minute or two later, very pleased with himself, the dog emerged with a possum clenched in his jaws: dinner was sorted. Coonch casually drove on down a bank, over a river and onto Barry's property, where we stayed for four days.

When Barry started talking — that voice like gravel — we all listened intently as we knew we were in the presence of one of the great storytellers. Coonch was no different from the rest of us — he was mesmerised. But if Barry ever motioned there was something needing attention outside or an adventure around the corner, his sidekick and now best mate was instantly right there by his side.

It was no surprise to see on TV about a year later that Barry had written a new book, called *Wild Pork and Watercress,* about a grumpy middle-aged white guy and a young Maori boy who have a wonderful adventure. Many were saying it was Barry's finest work in years. He gave me a copy, and it's still my favourite.

Thirty years after its first publication, we're very fortunate to have another great storyteller take Barry's novel and turn it into an epic Kiwi adventure: it's funny, heart-warming and thrilling. Taika Waititi has written a wonderful screenplay and, combined with his great vision, he has directed what we hope will become a classic. I was lucky enough to see a few minutes of the movie before it went to editing and was left very excited and eager to return to my father's novel.

— *Martin Crump*

Barry Crump

ABOUT BARRY CRUMP

Barry Crump (1935–96) wrote over twenty semi-autobiographical books and became a media icon, epitomising the yarning Kiwi bushman. His works sold over a million copies in New Zealand alone, plus several hundred-thousand copies overseas — an astounding number that confirms him as one of New Zealand's most popular authors. In 1994 he received an MBE for his contribution to the arts.

John Barrie Crump — known as Barry — was born into a share-milking family in Papatoetoe, South Auckland. He would later describe his upbringing as tough. Crump was one of six children, all of whom were expected to help out with the farm work. Their father was frequently violent towards them and to their mother. From a young age, Crump preferred the outdoors to the classroom, and was shifted around various South Auckland schools before he left Otahuhu College aged fifteen.

Initially Crump worked as a farm hand and bushworker, moving around the country from the Kaimanawa Forest to South Westland. In 1952, he started work for the Wildlife Branch of the Department of Internal Affairs as a deer-culler in the Urewera region, a job he would eventually embellish into his first and hugely successful book, *A Good Keen Man* (1960). Set in what was to become trademark

Crump country — the rugged, inaccessible New Zealand bush — it is a coming-of-age story of a teenager's first job reducing the spread of 'noxious' deer, which were blamed at the time for causing erosion. Crump's deadpan style delivered not just a lively story of deer-culling and hunting goats and pigs, but also plenty of humour along with wry observations on human nature.

The book's success led to what Crump called his "first venture into proper fiction" with a series of novels that included *Hang On a Minute Mate* (1961), *One of Us* (1962) and *There and Back* (1963). The central character of these three books is the anti-hero Sam Cash, a cynical, yarn-spinning vagabond who takes up all manner of odd jobs — from fencing to farming, from timber-felling to mustering and breaking horses — in an effort to escape suburban monotony and responsibilities.

It was after two years' crocodile-hunting and sailing through northern Australia that Crump conceived his next book, *Gulf* (1964), later re-published under the title *Crocodile Country* (1990). *Gulf* achieved broad success, its Russian translation purportedly selling over 100,000 copies.

From 1960, Crump published a book almost every year until 1972, including collections of short stories such as *Warm Beer and Other Stories* (1969), *A Good Keen Girl* (1970) — which was a female spin-off of *A Good Keen Man* — and *Bastards I Have Met* (1971). The latter was written after Crump decided that bastards outnumbered heroes by about 15,000 to one, so he set about cataloguing them in an ABC of Bastardry, with such examples as the bad bastard, the clever bastard, the good bastard, the miserable bastard and, one of his favourite targets, the officious bastard.

Crump underwent a period of disillusionment in the early 1970s and would not write another book until 1980. It was spiritual enlightenment from his 1970s motorcycle ride through the UK, Europe, Turkey, Afghanistan and India that resuscitated Crump from what he identified as boredom with success. In India he had stayed with a Kashmiri family, where what he learnt further reinforced the same anti-materialist principles he embraced as part of his bushman identity. Crump officially joined the Baha'i faith on his return to New Zealand in 1982, though restlessness continued to punctuate his career.

Crump had acted in a film and worked as a television presenter for *Town and Around* in the 1960s, performing sketches and hosting interviews. In the early 1980s, he was to become even more recognisable as the advertising face for Toyota's four-wheel-drive vehicles. These television advertisements capitalised on Crump's reputation as a laconic bushman, and often featured comedic songs, one of which went on to be Team New Zealand's theme song in the 1992 America's Cup. It was around this time that Crump and his then wife, Robin, began 'Bush Telegraph', a talkback radio show that soon rose to popularity.

From the 1980s, Crump returned to writing books, including various reissues and compilations of his previous titles, as well as the new novels *Shorty* (1980), *Puha Road* (1982), *Wild Pork and Watercress* (1986) and *Bullock Creek* (1989), all of which echo stages and significant places in Crump's life. Labelled by one reviewer as 'Crump's masterpiece', *Wild Pork and Watercress* was set in Crump's beloved Urewera country. It sold out its initial print run of 12,500 copies within three days of publication, and by 1991 had sold 95,000 copies. Like many of his works, it was published in multiple subsequent editions.

Just as in his early publications, Crump's later novels continued to offer his simple, direct narrative voice, his humour, his characters that were typically as "sharp as a sack-needle and as tough as a wool-pack", his descriptions of bushcraft and survival skills, and his depictions of life away from the rat race in a world reminiscent of the 1950s. However, Crump also started writing for a much younger audience: a poem for children was published as *Mrs Windyflax and the Pungapeople* in 1983 and was followed by several other Pungapeople stories. His adult poetry also appeared for the first time, included alongside stories in *Barry Crump's Bedtime Yarns* in 1988, and was the focus of *Song of a Drifter and Other Ballads* (1996). In the introduction to the latter book, Kevin Ireland commented that 'Crump's words belong to an agelong tradition of ballads and songs.'

Crump released the first of an autobiographical trilogy in 1992. *The Life and Times of a Good Keen Man* (1992) was followed by *Forty Yarns and a Song* (1994) and *Crumpy's Campfire Companion* (1996). Over his lifetime, Crump was married five times and had nine sons. One marriage was to the poet Fleur Adcock, another to novelist Jean Watson. On being awarded an MBE in 1994 for his services to and achievement in literature, Crump joked it would look a "hard case" pinned to his Swanndri. He died after a heart attack two years later, aged sixty-one. Soon after, family and friends released a selection of his prose and poetry in a memoir, *Tribute to Crumpy* (1997).

Crump's work lives on not just in book form but also in films. His short stories "Lawful excuse", "Time flies", "Hokonui Hank" and his novel *Hang On a Minute Mate* have been adapted for the screen. The latter was also adapted into a play by Anthony McCarten in 1992. In a newspaper interview about the play, Crump said, "It's still a part of the tapestry of New Zealand life. I still live a bit like that." A film of *Wild Pork and Watercress* had been planned when Crump was still alive, but he did not like the screenplays and it never eventuated. After Crump's death, Taika Waititi bought the rights to the book, drafted the screenplay, and became the film's director as well as one of its producers. As he told *The New Zealand*

Herald, his vision for the film was to "start a resurgence of entertaining New Zealand films — adventure films like *Came a Hot Friday* and *Goodbye Pork Pie*, where people are fighting against the system but in a fun way. We've lost a bit of that in our filmmaking, we've been really dark and arty." He cast Sam Neill and Julian Dennison in the lead roles, along with an impressive line-up of other actors.

Of the original novel, *The New Zealand Herald* quoted Waititi as saying, "It's a quick read, really engaging, and I recommend it to everyone. It's so entertaining, quite beautifully written and profound. Everyone thinks Barry Crump was just a hunting man but his writing is very good. It's simple, and I don't mean simple as in not having any substance, but a minimalist style, straight to the point. Hemingway also had a minimalist style and that's the kind of writing I like: not flowery and over the top, but straight up. There's something for everyone there."

The film's release comes twenty years after Crump's death and thirty years after the book's first publication.

CHAPTER
ONE

THE WIFE'S
SISTER'S BOY

My proper name's Richard Morehu Baker but they always call me Ricky. My mother was quarter-Maori and I was born in 1974, years later and a lot darker-skinned than my brother and sister, and don't let anyone tell you *that* doesn't make a difference. I always had trouble fitting in. People were always getting a surprise to find out I actually belonged in our family. I was also a bit overweight and not much good at sports and stuff like that.

By the time I'd been at school for a few years I could read miles better than most of the other kids but I wasn't much good at anything else, and they decided I was a slow learner. They shifted me around from class to class, trying to work out where fat Maori boys who can't play rugby or learn simple stuff fitted in. I knew they had me all wrong, but there wasn't much I could do about it.

I've always been able to remember just about anything I want to and it's easy for me to learn things. Too easy. I was worried about all the stuff that was going into my head, and they were shoving more in all the time. The wrong sort of stuff, too. I couldn't forget a lot of it. I used to be scared my head was going to fill up till it couldn't take any more and I'd suddenly go mad, or burst or something. So I took time off school, which I usually had to pay for with more trouble. But heads are only so big.

Anyway, while all this was going on my parents got divorced and my mother took custody of me, mainly because nobody seemed to know exactly where my father was living. He was never allowed in the house when he'd been drinking, and he just did more and more drinking till he didn't come home at all. Things got worse at home and school until in the end my mother couldn't handle me. Looking back, I seem to have spent a lot of time standing in various offices while adults sat around deciding what was going to happen to me next. I soon found out that thin white difficult boys are easier to "do something with" than overweight brown ones.

When I was nine they stuck me in a kind of health camp, but I couldn't stand it and got out of there as soon as I saw a chance. They caught up with me sneaking onto a bus to Wellington to stow away on a boat or plane to Australia, and I was carted off to a social welfare home for delinquent boys which was worse than the health camp and trickier to get out of. I had to spend three nights there before I could get away, but I made it home and decided to hang on there as long as possible. The social welfare people found out I was there and came round a few times, but they left me there.

By this time my mother was getting ready to get married again. My stepfather-to-be liked it better when I wasn't around, but he did his best not to let on about it. My mother used to say that everything was going to be all right and we pretended along like that, but less than a year later I was back in a social welfare home for shoplifting a bag of potato chips. They locked us up in that place and I had a lot of trouble getting away. They found out I was back at home but they left me alone. I think my new stepfather might have stuck up for me that time. He was still trying to like me, and I was getting better at keeping my head down.

The next time they picked me up I was riding a ten-speed bike I didn't even know was supposed to be stolen. I ended up in the same place as before but they were watching me this time and it was nearly a month before I got a chance to get away. I was on the loose for seven weeks — joined up with a bunch of kids who were living in a burnt-out bus near Taupo. They didn't really want me around, either. I was too inexperienced, they reckoned, and I might bring attention to them. We were living off what we could steal out of houses and cars and shops, so I don't suppose I could blame them really.

It didn't last long, anyway. They busted in on us in the middle of the night and carted us all off to the police station, then after a long car ride in the early hours to a prison place, where they locked us up in cells. There was no way of getting out of there. Things were getting worse. This was actual prison.

It turned out that I was too young to stay there, and after four days they got me in this office and told me I was being given one last chance to straighten myself up. I didn't deserve it, the social welfare man reckoned, but if I agreed to co-operate my Uncle Hector and Aunt Bella Faulkner had offered to take me into fostership on a trial basis and wasn't that wonderful of them.

The bloke was lying. Uncle Hec would never have offered to take anyone like me in. He didn't even like kids. It was another shove-around without me being consulted about it. But being in jail's no joke either, so I said all right, and the next day I was delivered to Uncle Hec and Aunty Bella's farm at the end of a windy stony road, eighty-seven kilometres from Gisborne. At this stage, I was twelve years and three weeks old.

The Faulkners' farm was up a valley beside a river called the Apopo, and everything about the place was old and falling to bits.

You could tell where their place started by all the thistles and scrub everywhere. Their road fence was all overgrown with briar bushes and long grass and they had a rusty old drum on a post with their name on it near the front gate. Two muddy wheel tracks went curving up the hill to their rusty old blue car parked outside the house, which was surrounded by falling rails and a skimpy hedge, with weeds and long grass growing right up to the window-sills round one side and the back. On the other side was Aunty Bella's vegetable garden. There was a path trodden in the grass between the gate and the back porch.

The Apopo river was about a hundred metres from the house, and the old woolshed with its rusty corrugated iron and red-streaked mossy boards was out on the flat between. It was a skin shed, a toolshed, a workshop — it was the only other building on the place apart from the house and everything happened down there. Uncle Hec used to spend a lot of time sitting on a staple-box with a folded sack nailed onto it for padding, tipped back against the wall of the shed, looking up the valley.

The river was quite a big one, stony and shingly and about twenty metres across at the crossings, with deep pools in between. Upstream Uncle Hec's 140 acres went steeply up from the river flats, which were covered with clumps of blackberry and other scrub. Patches of grass were still quite numerous around the bottoms of the ridges, but higher up there was just manuka and gorse with streaks of new bush in the gullies. Beyond that dark ridges of native bush went right up to a broken blue range shaped like a train crash. It was real steep. From the shed you could see where little streams came falling down between the ridges to make Rough Creek, which ran into the Apopo up at the end of the "Property".

It was an interesting place all right. I'd been there a few times before this, visiting. Uncle Hec was usually taking it easy and Aunty Bella was usually very busy. Aunty Bella was my mother's eldest sister and it was she who'd set up the taking me into fostership thing. I could tell by the way she called me a poor lamb and was inclined to do a bit too much hair-ruffling and cuddling and stuff. She was going to supervise me on correspondence school.

Aunty Bella's was the best place to be hungry I ever knew. I'll tell you more about that later. She always wore slacks and cardigans and had her grey-black hair in a big clip at the back to keep it out of her way. When Aunty Bella was angry she'd call you a scallywag, whatever that was. It wasn't as serious as Uncle Hec getting angry, that's for sure.

Uncle Hec was very old. Over fifty. He called himself a bushman but it was hard to tell exactly what that meant. Most of the family used to say he was a no-hoper, when they talked about him at all. I'd picked up that he'd been in prison for "something disgraceful" when he was young. Another time I'd heard that it was for fighting. He was a grouchy old codger and most of the kids were a bit scared of him. He was supposed to be real stubborn when it came to an argument. He'd had a difference of opinion with the electricity people a few years before and they'd cut the power off, so Uncle Hec told them to come and take their poles and wire off his place. There was a story about him getting a big fine for cutting down their poles with a chainsaw. He was tall and thin with bony knuckles and hairy blue eyes and only bottom teeth.

That was really all I knew about Uncle Hec and Aunty Bella at the time I was dumped there, except that Uncle Hec had the most terrific way of shutting up my mother I ever saw. She never did approve of Uncle Hec, and just when she was getting wound up telling him what a lazy pig he was and how her sister deserved better, Uncle Hec would spit. Right past her. She never finished what she was saying. Not once. You wouldn't have been surprised either, if you'd seen Uncle Hec spit.

They had a daughter, cousin Judy. I'd only seen her a few times. She was a nurse, married to a doctor and living in Africa. She used to send letters describing the atrocious conditions where they lived. I was given Judy's old room next to the kitchen.

Uncle Hec wasn't exactly overwhelmed with joy about me being there at first, so I wasn't exactly overwhelmed with joy about him either. As far as he was concerned I was just the wife's sister's boy from the city and had to be put up with for the time being, till I ran away again or something. But at least Aunty Bella wanted me around.

One of the best things about the Faulkners' place was all the animals. They had eleven chooks and a rooster called Dreyfus, who ran around free-range and perched in the big macrocarpa at night. We were always looking around for where the chooks were laying this time. There were four muskovy ducks half-wild in the swamp across the river among the wild ducks and wekas and pukekos. There were rabbits up the river flats, and hares too. Sometimes bunches of wild goats would come down out of the bush to feed in the fern above the house. There were wild pigs up the back, and deer — Uncle Hec had shot a spiker with his shotgun when he was pheasant-shooting a few weeks before. Its skin with a big hole in it was hanging on a rafter in the shed.

There were supposed to be 250 sheep on the place, but there weren't that many left. I think Uncle Hec used to add one every time we ate one. Two horses called Mack and Rosie lived up the flats and wouldn't let anyone catch them. There were also about thirty big calves living in the scrub up the valley, getting fattened up for "the sale".

I decided to have a good try at fitting in with them. I was worried about the way things were going between me and the social welfare people, so I started off doing everything I was told. And that was plenty — they expected me to pull my weight. Uncle Hec would tell me what I had to do and show me how to do it. Once. After that I was supposed to know all about it. But in spite of that it didn't take me long to work out how to live there and keep out of most of the trouble.

Uncle Hec would get up just after the rooster crowed in the morning and give me a yell. "Okay, Ricky!"

I could never figure out why we had to get up so early in the morning and then loaf around all day hardly doing anything, but that's the way they wanted it, so I went along with them.

Uncle Hec would have a wash at the tubs and I'd get dressed and take the bucket from upside-down on the bench and go out to find the house cow, Sally, who was always somewhere down at the far end of the paddock. I'd chase her up to the shed and into the bail at the side, wash her udder and milk her with big musical squirts into the frothy bucket. It's handy to know how to milk a cow. Nothing to it really, and the cream you get is like no other cream. And, while I'm doing this, smoke would come pouring out of the chimney over at the house. Sometimes it would hang in a blue streak right along the valley.

When I came in and put the milk on the bench Uncle Hec would be getting around in his long-johns making a pot of tea. I'd have a wash at the tubs on the porch and dry my hands and face on the big towel hanging there. By the time we were on our second cups of tea Aunty Bella would come out and start rattling things around, and all we had to do then was keep out of her way. Uncle Hec would be ordered to go and dress himself decently and I was always asked if I'd had my wash yet.

"Yep," I'd say.

"There's a lamb," she'd say.

I'd sit at the table with a book and Uncle Hec would come in tucking his shirt into his pants and start fiddling with the old battery radio to get *Morning News*, and grumble between the reports that "they're going bloody mad out there". And then the smells of rolled oats floating in cream and brown with sugar, and wild-pork bacon and bright orange free-range eggs and toast would take our minds off everything else. Good breakfasts, those ones.

Around eight o'clock Uncle Hec and I and the chook-bucket would get chased out of the house. We might decide to stack lengths of manuka into the rack and cut a pile of wood for the stove with Uncle Hec's old chainsaw. Sometimes we'd take the Winchester rifle up the flats and shoot some rabbits for dinner. One each. Or we might have a possum in one of the traps in the old orchard and hang its skin on a board with the others in the shed. Or we might just go down the shed and sit around. Depended mainly what mood Uncle Hec was in. For instance, not long after I came there (four weeks and two days, actually), we were down at the shed and I said, "How come you never have to do much work, Uncle Hec?"

"Because I'm the most successful farmer around, that's why."

"How come your farm's in such a mess, then?"

"Mess?" he said, looking around. "Where?"

"Well, all those prickles and bushes along the road fence," I said.

"That's rose-hip," he said, as though he'd grown it there on purpose. "Great stock-food, the old rose-hip. Loaded with vitamin C, lasts right through the winter. Valuable stuff to have around, that."

I watched him carefully. I was suspicious of Uncle Hec. When I was six he'd told me he had a sheep's lung in him because one of his had been ripped out by a flying crowbar in an explosion. He even had a big scar across his ribs to prove it, and I'd believed him for more than a year before I'd made a fool of myself telling them at school about it. I looked around. The only tidy thing on the whole place, outside the house, was the vegetable garden — Aunty Bella's garden.

"What about all the clumps of weeds and stuff all over the paddocks?" I said, pointing up the river flats.

"They're not weeds, that's blackberry. Good tucker, the old blackberry. The rabbits like it, too. If I cleared off all the blackberry I'd have to go all the way up to Goat Gully to get meself a feed. Anyway it's not worth doing too much to this place. The Forestry's supposed to be going to buy up all the land around here and plant it in pines."

"Sounds like a good excuse for being lazy," I said.

"Not too lazy to leap up and flatten any young buggers who get too cheeky with me," he said.

"You'd better not hit me," I told him.

"Then you'd better not get cheeky with me," he said, getting up off his box.

We were standing there like that, looking at each other, when the gong started ringing for me to go up to the house for correspondence. Must have been ten o'clock.

The gong was a big round piece of metal off some old farm machine, hanging on a wire in the macrocarpa tree by the side gate. Aunty Bella used to bang it with a piece of pipe when it was time to eat or when Uncle Hec was wanted up at the house. Sometimes you could hear it down at the Hickeys' place, nearly a mile away. Just as well it rang when it did that day. I didn't know what Uncle Hec meant by "flatten" at that stage.

At ten o'clock every weekday I had to go up to the house and do schoolwork. If Aunty Bella hadn't taken it so seriously I'd have been dangerously bored by those lessons, but she was so good about it I had to try and not disappoint her. The worst hassle was writing it all down neat enough for them. I actually started waking up to some of the things they'd been trying to tell me at school. Correspondence is the best kind of school for people who have trouble fitting in. You get left alone more.

While I finished the schoolwork Aunty Bella would put lunch on.

Then I'd go and gong real loud for Uncle Hec and we'd have lunch. It might be cold roast mutton with Aunty Bella's special chutney, and salad from the garden and big slices of oven bread and butter. And cups of tea. Stuff like that. As much as you wanted. Pretty good.

After lunch we usually had a lie on our beds for an hour or two. I read books mostly, especially science fiction if I could get my hands on any. They had hardly any books at the Faulkners', and nothing any good. Aunty Bella joined the library in town for me and I read everything I could borrow around the neighbours.

Around two-thirty or three o'clock Aunty Bella would get active and noisy again, and after a cup of tea or two Uncle Hec and I would drift outside and maybe bring in a load of firewood, or put a post in a gap in a fence, or some other half-necessary job. After an hour or two of this Uncle Hec would move off towards his seat down at the shed. I sometimes felt like going for a walk and exploring around the place. I especially liked climbing up the hills to a high place. It sometimes gave me a kind of free feeling I'd never noticed anywhere else. By this time of day Uncle Hec and I had often seen enough of one another — I could usually tell.

Dinner at night meant another wash and the kitchen full of smells and activity, with pot lids rattling and steaming on the stove, and something smoking and spitting whenever Aunty Bella opened the oven door and stabbed in with her big fork, all the time giving orders like the captain on the bridge of a star-ship. Uncle Hec would probably be grumbling about the quality of the mantles they make these days as he lit the kerosene pressure-lamp.

Then the hot plates of stuffed braised rabbit, a whole one each and one extra, with thick brown oniony gravy and roasted kumara from the garden and fluffy mashed potato — as much as you could eat. Then a third of a big blackberry pie hidden under cream skimmed off this morning's milk in lumps as big as your spoon.

"Please may I leave the table," I'd say.

"Yeah, you'd better get out of here before you bust," Uncle Hec said one night.

"Hector!" said Aunty Bella. "You mustn't say things like that. Ricky's a growing boy."

"He's growing all right," said Uncle Hec. "Outwards. Look at the size of him."

"At least I'm not a skinny old bag of bones like you," I shouted at him.

He put both hands on the table to leap up and flatten me, but Aunty Bella said, "Now that's quite enough from both of you. Ricky, off you go and run the bath. And put those clothes in the wash, they're filthy. You're not wearing them another day."

I'd lie in the bath listening to Uncle Hec trying to get the radio adjusted right and finally leaving it half off the station. Aunty Bella would clatter through the washing up while I'd dry myself on a towel hot from the rack over the stove and get into my pyjamas before drying the dishes and putting them away properly. Then I'd sip a mug of Milo made with hot milk, cop a cuddle from Aunty Bella, and brush my teeth.

"Good night," I'd say.

"Good night, lamb. Now don't you go reading all hours of the night. You'll ruin your eyes."

"Okay, goodnight."

Uncle Hec would grunt. He doesn't like saying things like hello or goodbye or good morning or good night.

I'd light my candle and get into bed, discovering that Aunty Bella had put a hot water bottle in my bed while I was having my bath. I'd discovered that a scallywag is someone who peels the potatoes too thick. I'd read for an hour or so. Around nine-thirty Uncle Hec would grumble his way off to bed saying there's never anything decent on the bloody wireless these days. The last sounds in the house would be Aunty Bella clattering around getting everything ready for the morning. A clank of the milk bucket upside-down on the bench and the day would be over.

I'd pinch out my candle and lie there in the dark, listening to the Apopo river talking away to itself in mangled voices beyond the window, and working out the best way of running away from there — just in case I needed to later on.

CHAPTER
TWO

A DOG
LIKE ZAG

There's quite a lot I haven't mentioned about the Faulkners and their funny old overgrown farm. For example Uncle Hec had this dog, a black-and-white Border Collie cross called Zag. It used to follow Uncle Hec everywhere when it was off the chain but it didn't like anyone else even patting it. A one-man dog, Uncle Hec said it was. I didn't like Zag much at first because he wouldn't let me be friends with him, but that was before I found out he was a champion dog. It was an important day for me, that.

After breakfast Uncle Hec said, "You'd better stick those new boots of yours on today, young feller. We'll see if we can walk some of that surplus condition off you."

"What are we going to do?" I asked him.

"I want to go up to the end of the property and see how many of the cattle I can find. If there's any fat enough we'll bring 'em down and stick 'em in the front paddock for the sale. They must be getting pretty big by now."

We took Zag, who seemed to know there was something on. He

dashed around everywhere and jumped up on Uncle Hec till he got growled at. It looked to me as though Zag must have been flattened a few times, the way he instantly obeyed Uncle Hec, but I found out later that those dogs are like that.

We had to cross the river six times and you had to watch where you were putting your feet on the wet stones. I was having to hurry to keep up and thinking we must be near the end of the property by this time, when Uncle Hec suddenly stopped and I nearly ran into him.

"That's fresh pig-rooting up there," he said quietly, pointing up a ferny ridge to a scattered patch of dug-up dirt amongst the fern. "They mightn't be too far away."

And he stood squinting up the ridge.

"Shall we go back and get the rifle?" I suggested.

"We might be able to stop one with the dog if we get lucky," he said. "I haven't got a knife on me, have you got that one of yours?"

"Yep," I said, pulling it out of my pocket and opening it up. "It's sharp, too."

"Put it away," he said, "and stay close behind me. We'll climb up to that rooting and see if the dog can pick up a fresh scent."

We climbed up from the river and pushed our way up a faint track through the high fern, and before we reached where the rooting was Zag started getting excited, trying to push past Uncle Hec in the fern.

"Okay, go on," he said, and Zag shot away up the ridge.

"They must be pretty close," Uncle Hec whispered. "We'd better get off this track in case he brings 'em this way."

I got quickly into the fern behind him, and just then there was a terrific crashing and snarling and whoofing just up ahead of us. We could hear pigs crashing off around both sides of the ridge. I saw the fern shake in a big ripple as one of them charged away, and I saw it for a moment as it ran round into the next gully. A big black one with long hair sticking up along its back. I don't mind admitting it made me a bit nervous to realise animals like *that* were running around the place — and there we were with only a dog and a pocket knife.

But that was nothing. Suddenly Zag was fighting and snarling and crashing and driving another one down through the fern and manuka in the gully on the other side.

"He's onto one," said Uncle Hec. "He might stop it in the river. We'd better get down there."

We ran after the dog and pig, crashing and rolling down through the fern, and when we slid down the bank onto the river stones here was this big black pig, going round and round in the water at the edge of the river with Zag hanging onto one of its ears.

"Quick," said Uncle Hec. "Give me the knife."

I pulled it out and he snatched it off me while I was still trying to get it open for him. He ran over and tried to get behind the pig, but just as he ducked in to grab it by the back leg the pig threw the dog off and turned on him.

I always regret I didn't see exactly what happened after that because I was too busy getting up the bank, but when I looked again Uncle Hec was standing in the river up to his knees and Zag had the pig by the ear again out on the stones. Round and round they went, the pig grunting and scoffing and squealing, with the dog snarling and shaking at it. I didn't know Zag could get so savage. I had respect for him over that.

Uncle Hec dived in again and this time he got the pig by the back leg and struggled and turned it over and stuck it in the neck with my knife. The pig's blood poured out on the stones, and even after it stopped kicking Zag had to be booted away from it. He kept wanting to get stuck in again.

"Good pig that," said Uncle Hec, breathing heavily and kicking Zag away again. "What say we singe it, eh?"

"Too right," I agreed, whatever singeing was.

Singeing was throwing a heap of dead manuka down onto the riverbed from a clump up the hill and lighting a big fire. When it was going properly we carried the pig across to the river and dunked it in until it was good and wet when we swung it onto the fire. The hairs sprang short in the flames with a steaming and sizzling and smell of burning. When the bottom side was well heated up we turned it over and scraped the burnt-off bristles with splinters of driftwood, and the whole outside layer of skin peeled away, leaving white skin underneath. When we'd scraped the whole pig we burnt a brown skin on it in the embers and lifted the hot tight carcase out onto the stones. And were we sweating! It's hot work, singeing wild pigs.

Uncle Hec gutted the pig with my knife, which was getting very blunt, and examined the liver. "Perfect," he said, and threw it into the hollow carcase.

We threw the rest of the guts into the fern at the foot of the bank and set off to pack the meat home. It weighed about twenty-five kilos, that pig, but I managed to carry it most of the way. We hung it in the big meat-safe under the lean-to behind the shed. Aunty Bella came down to have a look and pretended to be shocked at the mess we were in. "I think I'll make some brawn," she said.

"All right, eh," said Uncle Hec when we were sharing the soap under the tap.

"All right," I agreed.

I wanted a dog like Zag for my own. I'd decided to be a hunter, but I wasn't quite ready to discuss it with Uncle Hec yet.

Next morning, after a breakfast of liver, onions, eggs, tomatoes and toast, we cut our pig down the middle with the old hand-saw and cut it up on the kitchen bench into roasts and chops and stewing-meat. Then I got sent to two different neighbours with parcels of meat because we were the only ones in the valley without a fridge.

That was the best pork I'd ever tasted, and I've especially liked wild pork ever since — roast wild pork, with crackling and roast kumaras and pumpkin and gravy and watercress. I wanted a dog of my own all right. A pig-dog.

I liked doing things for Aunty Bella, she was a real good sort, and made the most beautiful brawn you've ever eaten. And she could turn a bucket of ordinary old mushrooms into the most delicious bacony creamy toast-soaking stuff you could imagine. She had a bit of magic, Aunty Bella. She was my best friend as well.

Not long after we got the pig (just under a week — okay, four days), we were sitting around down the shed waiting for the gong to go for dinner, and I said to Uncle Hec, "The Hickeys' bitch has got a litter of pups by Old Dave's black Labrador. Six of them."

"Yeah, I know," he said. "Those pups ought to be just about weaned by now."

"Yes," I said. "As a matter of fact Joe said I could have my pick out of three of them — that's if it's okay with you for me to have a dog."

I was watching him. He shook his head. "No way, mate. You're not bringing any Alsatian-Labrador dogs around here."

"Why not?" I asked. This was a bit embarrassing because I'd already told Joe Hickey Uncle Hec wouldn't mind.

"Because they're no bloody good, that's why," he said.

"You just don't want me to have a dog at all."

"You can have a dog, if you want one that bad, but you're not bringing any scoffing bloody wool-classers around here. If you can get the right kind of dog you can keep it, providing you look after it yourself. They have to be kept fed, you know."

"You'll only keep saying they're no good," I said.

"Only if they are no good," he said, and the gong went for us to go and have a wash for dinner — roast pork with all the trimmings.

I left it for a whole day and when we were down the shed again

I said to him, "How do you go about getting the right sort of dog, Uncle Hec?"

"You can never tell what a dog's going to turn out like," he said, "but you can eliminate some of the risks."

"How do you do that?"

"Well for a start you have to decide just what you want a dog for."

"Catching pigs, like Zag," I said.

"Well Zag's a cattle-dog, and I reckon they're as good in the bush as anything you'll get. Working dogs are light on their feet, that's important. They'll live on nothing, and life's always a lot easier if you don't have to worry about what your dog's up to. Something with a bit of working-dog in it'd probably do you."

"How do you find dogs like that?" I said.

"You keep your eyes and ears open, and check with me before you bring any home."

That was the best I was going to do for the time being, so I left it at that.

Not long afterwards (two days) I had another run-in with Uncle Hec. I'd dug the point of my knife into my hand and it wouldn't stop bleeding. I went round the shed and showed Uncle Hec. He twirled some cobweb out of the corner of the shed with a stick and put it on my cut hand. The bleeding stopped instantly. Magic.

"How did you do it?" he said.

"I must have put my knife in my pocket half-closed," I said.

"Not very smart, eh," he said, and sat down on his staple-box again.

"I'm smarter than most people," I told him.

"You're a bit smart," he admitted, and I watched him because he didn't usually admit things like that.

"I'm smarter than you, anyway," I said. "You can't even count 161 sheep."

He started getting up off his box and suddenly I was sitting on the ground with my hearing only just coming back in time to hear him say ". . . asking for that," as he walked off towards the house. I'd been flattened! I jumped up and grabbed a pair of fencing pliers that were sitting on a post and almost let him have it — just stopped myself in time. I'd never been hit like that before. I had extra respect for Uncle Hec over that. He could flatten you all right.

Another thing happened one night when we were coming back down the flats with some rabbits we'd just shot and I was carrying the rifle.

"How old do you think someone would have to be before they could shoot with a .22?" I asked him casually.

"Nothin' to do with age," he said.

"What, then?"

"It's how much brains y'got."

"I've got brains," I said.

"Then you've got to be able to skin or pluck and gut everything you shoot," he said.

It was I who skinned and gutted the rabbits that night. It wasn't as easy as Uncle Hec made it look, but I managed. I cut the heads and feet off them and took them up and gave them to Aunty Bella.

"Heavens," she said, "you've put them through the mincer."

But Uncle Hec had said I was "getting the message", which sounded okay to me.

After dinner that night I got the .22 out of the cupboard and got him to show me how it worked and how to hold it right. We pulled the whole thing to bits on the kitchen table in the finish, and I put it together again. Nothing much to it, really. I usually had to pretend to be dumber than usual when grown-ups were showing me how to do something.

Next day we had a shooting session down by the bend of the river.

We fired off two and a half packets of fifty, and by the finish I was putting three bullets in a five-inch group at seventy metres, which Uncle Hec said wasn't bad with open sights. He was good, though. In fact Uncle Hec was the best shot with a rifle I ever saw, which turned out to be very lucky for us a few times.

That night I heard Uncle Hec say to Aunty Bellà, "The young coot's not a bad shot," and I couldn't get out of the bath for grinning.

I lived for shooting rabbits for a while. There were dozens of them around and the older ones were getting cunning and hard to sneak up on. I missed a few, but I got a few as well. I thought I'd blown the whole thing one day when Uncle Hec met me at the gate and we were looking at a big hare I'd shot in the neck. I thought the rifle was on safety and pulled the trigger to test it, and it went off and blew a hole in the dirt between our feet.

We stood looking at each other like someone was going to flatten someone, and then he said, "If you ever do anything like that again you can put the rifle in the cupboard and leave it there."

"Yes, sir," I said. And meant it. It was hard to believe, getting away with that one. I wondered if Uncle Hec did something stupid like that with a rifle when he was a young bloke. You don't ask Uncle Hecs about things like that; they'd think it was personal.

It was the best fun so far, going out hunting on my own with the rifle. Uncle Hec had a .303 that just about knocked you over, and a shotgun with hammers you had to pull back to fire it. He didn't like me using the shotgun and I was happy with the .22.

"You can shoot anything you want with a .22, if you know what you're doin'," he said.

One day he sent me up to Goat Gully to get a goat for dog tucker. I got one just up the creek at the bottom of a slip — dropped it right where it was standing. I gutted it, carried it back and hung it in the dog-tucker tree near Zag's kennel and didn't even say anything to any uncles about it. A young billy-goat. As far as I was concerned that made me a hunter, but I didn't advise Uncle Hec about that just yet.

Around this time, just after I'd turned twelve and a half, I nearly came unstuck with my schoolwork. They wrote a letter saying they were so pleased with the standard of my work that they were considering putting me forward a whole year by stages. I was lucky having Aunty Bella on my side — she advised them against it because I was just settling down and any changes might set me back, and stuff like that. They left me alone for a while after that, but they always had me worried. Fat Maori boys can get into terrible trouble with those sorts of people. I was careful to get a few simple things wrong here and there after that.

A pair of hunters, the Shortage brothers, Bill and Norm, had access rights to hunt up the back of Uncle Hec's place. They came out most weekends during the winter and brought various mates and dogs with them. They usually always got a pig or two and sometimes a deer as well. They were well known for having a good pack of hunting dogs.

But they got Uncle Hec's back up in a big way one day. Their dogs came out of the bush ahead of them and cleaned up four of his sheep before they could stop them. Boy, he could sure get himself worked up, Uncle Hec. They offered to pay him for the sheep, but he didn't even hear them. They offered to shoot the two guilty dogs right there in front of him, but that made no difference either. He told them never to come back on the place with their scoffing bloody mongrels or he'd shoot the whole bloody lot of them.

We had a few arguments after that because he used to say the Shortages never even offered to pay him for the sheep their dogs killed, and I used to say they did offer but he hadn't heard them. He'd grunt and say, "Well I never heard 'em," but next time he'd be telling someone about it he'd still say the Shortages never even offered to pay for the sheep. You just have to give up on grown-ups on some things.

Anyway, just before all this happened Norm Shortage offered me one of his dogs. He had two of them out of the same litter — they were big fox-terriers crossed with a cattle-dog/red-setter bitch. They were ten and a half months old and just starting to hunt. Norm only wanted to keep one of them, so how would I like to have the other one?

Would I? I looked at the dog he was offering me and I liked it straightaway — red with white patches, nearly-prick-ears, bouncy, cheeky, real fast and intelligent-looking. His name was Willy.

"Here, Willy. Here, boy," I said, but it didn't take any notice of me.

"It'll take him a while to get used to you," said Norm, "but once he does you won't be able to kick him out of your road."

"I'll have to ask Uncle Hec first," I said. "He's a bit fussy about what kind of dogs we have around here. Is it okay if I let you know next weekend?"

"Sure," said Norm, ruffling my hair with his hand. "I'll bring him out again next Sunday, okay?"

I was so pleased I hardly even wanted to kick him one for ruffling my hair like that. I don't like people ruffling my hair. Someone was going to get a punch one of these days. Flattened.

During the week I softened Uncle Hec up till he had to tell me to shut up about the bloody dog.

"I'll let you know when I've had a look at it," he said.

On the Sunday Uncle Hec looked Willy over when he jumped out of the Shortages' trailer with their other four dogs. I was watching him, and after the longest time I'd ever waited he gave the smallest nod of his head I'd ever seen. Norm caught my dog for me and I took him on a piece of rope and tied him beside Zag along the hedge. That was the Sunday Uncle Hec's sheep got worried by the Shortages' dogs, so it was a close shave.

"What makes dogs kill sheep, Uncle Hec?" I asked him when he'd cooled down, two days later.

"They live in town and come out here to hunt. The dogs don't know the difference between a pig and a sheep, half of 'em. It's the bloody owners who need shootin', most of the time."

"How do you keep your dog from worrying sheep?"

"Get him used to them. Work them with him. Let him know you don't want him to bite 'em and he never will."

"Do you think Willy would worry sheep?"

"If he does it'll be *your* fault, and *he'll* get shot."

After that I took my dog everywhere I went. In fact most of the places I went were only so I could take him there, which meant a lot of rambling around the hills. Willy was a real obedient dog, and never even looked like chasing the sheep unless I put him round them. He took to hunting with Zag and we started catching good pigs with them from the beginning. It was the best fun ever. I got Uncle Hec to come hunting whenever I could wangle it, which was difficult to organise sometimes because he'd only hunt when we needed meat. I managed to give quite a lot of pork to the Hickeys and two other families further down the valley who all had freezers, and we usually went out on a proper pig hunt once every two weeks or so.

We'd go up-river and climb up a ridge we reckoned was likely to hold something, and we usually got a bit of action before we'd gone far. Willy developed into a neat little finder, and Zag would wait for Willy to bark on something and then nick round to head it off. They pulled off some good ones, working together like that, and we hardly ever came back without "something for the pot", as Uncle Hec used to say.

One morning when I was looking around for Sally the house cow

I thought I saw a half-grown black pig trot through a little clearing in the manuka above the house. It was only just getting daylight and it was about as far as you could see, but I let the dogs off and ran up the flat to get ahead of where the pig looked to be heading.

We'd just come round into the first gully past the house when Willy got a scent on the wind and shot up into the scrub. There were two barks when he found it, only about sixty yards up the side, and then a squeal when he turned it round and brought it crashing down and out into the open. When the pig saw Zag it swerved away towards the shed with both dogs catching up on it. They spun it round and stopped it by the woodblock. Willy got on one ear and Zag got on the other and that pig just had to stand there squealing.

Uncle Hec in his long-johns got there just before I did. He pulled the axe out of the woodblock and donged the pig on the head with the back of it and kicked the dogs away. My knife was in my other pants and we had to yell out to Aunty Bella to bring one down from the house. She arrived in her dressing-gown and slippers and I grabbed the knife off her and stuck the pig, which was starting to come round. It was a young boar, about sixty pounds, Uncle Hec reckoned, and we singed it right there beside the woodblock.

"That dog of yours might just turn out all right," said Uncle Hec as we scraped the burning hair.

"He's all right, all right," I said.

"He could turn out all right," he said again.

At that stage neither of us could have guessed how important it was going to be to us that Willy turned out all right.

CHAPTER
THREE

OTHER
PEOPLE

By the time I was thirteen I could do most of the things Uncle Hec could around the farm, though he would never have admitted it. According to him I always sharpened the chainsaw wrong, or gave the dogs the wrong whistle, or used too much oil on his good sharpening-stone, or deliberately made the horses hard to catch. It was always my fault when we missed out on a pig or deer because if I was on the ridge I should have been in the creek, and if I was in the creek I should have been on the ridge. And all this was supposed to be because I was so fat.

He was hard to live with all right, but in spite of that, Uncle Hec and I were getting along a bit easier than at first. We still had to be careful not to get into a confrontation — we didn't want to have to find out who'd give in first, I suppose. He used to get on my nerves by always referring to how fat I was, especially in front of other people, and I used to get on his nerves by running around the side of the house and jumping on the loose board on the porch. It could shake the whole house when I hit it right, but even if Aunty Bella shouted with fright, Uncle Hec never let on he'd noticed it. I could tell it got him rattled, though.

Aunty Bella was just the opposite. According to her I never did anything wrong.

"He'd bust a bloody anvil," Uncle Hec would say.

"He's a growing boy," she'd say. "It's just a stage he's going through, isn't it, lamb?" and she'd ruffle my hair and give me a squeeze.

The main thing about Uncle Hec and Aunty Bella, though, was that they liked each other. They were friends, better than any other old people I'd ever known before. It was worth putting up with a lot of other grown-up stuff for that. What kept me from running away from there when things got bad was the way Uncle Hec never cared about my Maori skin. Fat white boys are always less embarrassing to have around than fat brown boys, I knew that, but it never seemed to bother Uncle Hec one way or the other. It was a long time before I gave up expecting him to say something about my Maoriness in an argument, because people like him always do, but he never did. It was a bit of a mystery to me, that.

Aunty Bella didn't count because she was quarter-Maori herself, and she wouldn't have been prejudiced about anything like that anyway. Being accepted by both of them in that kind of way was so good it got scary at times — almost like fitting in.

But the hunting was always the best fun. I usually forgot about everything else when we were out with the dogs, walking through the bush and waiting for that first bark when they made a find. One day they chased a big hind right past me in a narrow creek, and I got such a surprise I didn't think of shooting until it was disappearing around the corner. I've been waiting for the next one to do that ever since.

≈

So, taking it all round, things were pretty good living at the Faulkners'. It was hard to believe the news that was coming over the radio and in the newspapers — hundreds of farmers walking off their farms and going on the dole, gangs and violence and police teams everywhere in the towns, the army running some of the country and the police running the rest, and the people ripping off everything they could get away with. Not much wonder we hardly ever went past the store and post office out on the main road these days.

"They're going bloody mad out there," Uncle Hec would say, and switch off the wireless to save the battery for the next lot of bad news.

It seemed as though everyone was having troubles except us, and then all ours landed on us at once. I was down at the Hickeys' place that day, helping them press some bales of wool, and Mrs Hickey came down to the woolshed and said that Aunty Bella had been taken ill and Uncle Hec had gone with her into the Gisborne hospital. I knew right then that something real bad was happening.

Uncle Hec was going to ring up later and let us know how Aunty Bella was. I was supposed to stay at the Hickeys' that night but I didn't want to. I went home and lit the lamp and had something to eat but I don't remember what it was. I couldn't even read that night — I just kind of knew that things were going to be different from now on.

Uncle Hec arrived home the next afternoon with Mrs Hickey. They were looking for me up at the house, but I was down the shed, sitting on Uncle Hec's staple-box, looking up the valley. Aunty Bella had died at five-thirty that morning. She'd had a stroke. And that was that.

Nothing could have been the same after that. I don't know about Uncle Hec, but I couldn't see across the gap Aunty Bella left in our lives. It should have happened to someone else, not us.

We made it to the funeral in the rusty blue car in spite of Uncle Hec's dangerous driving, and stood around feeling out of place among the relatives and other strangers — hard to tell which was which, and it was nothing to do with Aunty Bella being gone. My mother was living in Australia somewhere and they hadn't been able to contact her. One lady, some sort of cousin, ruffled my hair and said, "Poor thing, I wonder what's going to happen to *you* now."

After the funeral I had to wait for about an hour in the car while Uncle Hec had a private talk with some of his relatives. Neither of us talked all the way home — Uncle Hec's driving takes your mind off most other things anyway.

Uncle Hec took it all well, considering, but it was a bad time for both of us. It was worse because we hadn't realised how much stuff Aunty Bella had been doing around the place until we had to do it ourselves — things like winding up the clock, cleaning out the stove, or filling the water-tank.

After about six weeks, just when we were getting used to our own cooking, other people interfered in my life again. A letter came from the Social Welfare, addressed to Uncle Hec, which smelt like trouble to me. I read it out to him. ". . . *deeply sorry to learn of your recent sad bereavement, however in the light of the altered circumstances the situation with regard to the fostership of Richard Morehu Baker will naturally have to be reviewed. A Mr Draper will be calling on you in the near future to advise you what arrangements have been made . . .*"

"What does it mean?" I said.

Uncle Hec tapped the letter on the kitchen table with his finger.

"It means that you have to go back into one of those welfare homes until they can find another foster home for you, by the look of it," he said.

"Like hell I do," I said, jumping up. "I'm not going into any welfare home."

"You've got no choice," he said.

"Why can't I just stay here?"

"They wouldn't let you, not without a woman in the place."

"You just don't want me here, do you?"

"No, mate," he said. "Sit down. There's something I haven't told you about yet."

"What?" I didn't like the sound of all this.

"I can't stay here either."

"What do you mean?"

"You remember at the funeral, I got pulled aside by Wilf and Humphrey and them?"

"Yes."

"Well what they were telling me was that they've decided to sell the farm."

"*This* farm?"

"Yeah, this one."

"But it's *your* farm."

"It's a family property. Our folks left it equally between me and my two brothers and our sister — that's your Aunt Daphne. I was the only one interested in running the place so Bella and I took it over. Now the others want to sell up and split the money."

"But can they do that without you wanting to?"

"Sure, I wouldn't stop them. They reckon my share of the money'll buy me one of those nice little single units in town, where they can keep an eye on me."

"What are you going to do about it?"

"I think I'll take to the scrub for a spell. Trap a few skins, sell a bit of meat."

Aunty Bella had said how Uncle Hec used to disappear into the bush for weeks on end.

"I'm coming with you," I decided. "If we can stay in the bush till I'm fifteen they'll have to leave me alone."

"You can't come with me. You're still under the Social Welfare."

"No I'm not," I said. "I'm under you, and if you're going into the bush I'm coming too."

"Like hell you are. Forget it. It's out of the question."

That night we were still yelling back and forth in the dark between our rooms.

"Like hell you are," was the last thing Uncle Hec said about it, just before he started snoring.

It was very important to me not to get into the hands of the Social Welfare people again.

"Like hell you are," said Uncle Hec at breakfast next morning.

"You're not putting me in any institution."

"It's not *me* who's putting you anywhere."

"You are, by not taking me with you."

"I'd be breaking the law."

"Not if we leave before they officially change things. There's nothing to stop us having a spell in the bush if we want to."

"Forget it, you're wasting your breath."

That afternoon two men in a car came and stuck a FOR SALE sign on the front fence, and that sort of put the lid on it all. It was actually happening, Uncle Hec was right. The only thing for us to do was take to the bush.

"Like hell you are," said Uncle Hec that night. "I'm leaving for the Mangatoatoa hut as soon as they come and get you, so you might as well get used to the idea."

"You won't get into any trouble. I'll tell them I came of my own accord. I know how to run away — I've done it before, you know."

"You haven't done anything like this before."

"I can handle it, Uncle Hec. True."

"You don't know what you're talking about. Forget it."

Well, it was the hardest argument I ever won, and I had to risk a flattening before he finally gave in and said he'd have to think about it. I had to agree to a lot of stuff that would have to be rearranged later on, but he finally said it.

"We'll get away first thing tomorrer mornin'."

Left me exhausted, that.

≈

We nailed up a box of stuff Uncle Hec wanted kept for him, mostly tools, and wrote "Faulkner" on it with a piece of raddle. Everything else got left just as it was, except that we opened all the gates on our way up the flats so the stock wouldn't starve. It was only an hour or so after daylight when we climbed up onto the spur beyond Goat Gully, heading for the top of the Rakawhaia Ridge. It was a long climb, that. Every now and then we'd stop for a breather and look back down through the mist at the little farm. No talking — I suppose we'd done enough of that in the past few days.

Plodding up through the bush behind Uncle Hec, with loaded packs and the rifle, and the two dogs in behind, I was doing a bit of thinking. It had been such a hassle getting Uncle Hec to let me come with him that I hadn't taken much notice of what we'd brought with us. It sure didn't seem to be much preparation for holding out in the bush for two or three years. My main worry was what we were going to eat.

It hadn't taken us long to pack what we did bring. I had an old pack-frame with a synthetic-fibre sack tied onto it with nylon cord — sleeping-bag, spare pants, singlet and socks. My knife was in my pocket and I had a few books. Most of the spare space I'd filled with food to keep us going. Mug, fork and spoon, a couple of extra books shoved down the side and my green Swanndri jacket tied on the top, and that was my load. About twenty kilos, Uncle Hec reckoned.

Uncle Hec had his hold pack, sleeping-bag, some clothes, a bit of rope, the tea-billy — too little in my opinion. We were carrying the .22 because it was the most versatile rifle. We had 279 bullets for it.

I was wearing my Casio digital watch that my mother had given me. It told the month, the day, the date, the hour, the minute and the second. Uncle Hec was inclined to sling off about it at first. Didn't need 'em, he reckoned, but later on that watch became so important to us that we carried it knotted in a plastic bag and carried it in the zip-pocket of Uncle Hec's pack to avoid it getting wet or damaged or lost.

We'd left a note under a bottle of tomato sauce on the kitchen table saying, GONE HUNTING. H. FAULKNER. R. BAKER.

We stopped on the top of the ridge and rested with our backs against a big beech tree and ate some bread and cheese. The dogs moved around, sniffing the wind. The last bits of mist and cloud were blowing through the trees and as far as we could see ahead of us were ridges of bush, nothing but bush, going blue in the distance. It was hard to imagine how anyone could find their way around in it without getting lost. Uncle Hec had been hunting and trapping in the Urewera since he was a boy and reckoned he knew it like the back of his hand, but I didn't trust his memory all that much. I'd seen Uncle Hec forget things almost as soon as they happened — but he was still my best bet.

"Are we in the Urewera yet?" I asked him.

"Yes," he said, waving a piece of bread and cheese towards it all. "What we've got here is about a million acres of unbroken native bush, with about fifty Forestry Department huts scattered through it. I think I can find most of 'em, and they have to keep some supplies in them in case of trampers getting lost and that. The hunting's pretty good in most places. It mightn't always be easy to stick a feed under our belts but we shouldn't starve."

"How far is it to this hut we're going to?" I asked him.

"I've done it in five hours from home," he said. "But we're not in any great hurry. We'll be there before dark."

About half an hour's walk along the Rakawhaia Ridge and we came across an old track, which no one had used for a long time. We followed this track for about three hours, getting deeper into strange bush all the time. This was the real thing all right — there was deer-sign everywhere, droppings and hoofprints, and we kept the dogs close in behind us. We needed them to catch pork for us and didn't want them burning themselves out chasing deer.

We trudged up the longest ridge I'd ever seen and down off the track into the head of a creek I found out later was the Mangatoatoa. The dogs dived over into a hook-grassy clearing in the trees and grabbed a skinny boar. I sat with my load against a tree and let Uncle Hec go down and deal with it. It was too skinny for eating so we left it there and carried on down the creek. The dogs were a bit easier to control now that they'd had a bit of exercise.

On we went, walking through a world of trunks and branches and stones and roots and vines. I could hardly lift my feet or tell up from down by the time we came to the first big forks of the creek, where the country got wider and flatter. My pack was hurting my shoulders and I was just about falling over when we dropped our loads and sat down on the grass against a log. I must admit that it was only thoughts of the Social Welfare department that was keeping me going. "How much further?" I said, almost in a coma from being so tired.

"About an hour down the creek. How are you going?"

"I'm all right," I told him.

"Let's have a brew-up," he said. "I could use something to eat."

Thoughts of food livened me up and we lit a driftwood fire and had mugs of sweet tea, with bread and cold mutton and some watercress we found in a backwater. I felt better after that, but I had to use thoughts of the Social Welfare to get my legs moving properly when we got going again.

We crossed the creek back and forth from flat to flat, cutting across bush terraces with groves of big trees and waist-deep ferns until we came to the Mangatoatoa hut, where a big side creek came in on the right. It was the same as most of the Forestry huts in the Urewera, Uncle Hec said. Painted orange, tin roof and sides, one room with wooden bunks around the walls and a fireplace in one side. Table and shelves, a big locked food-cupboard broken open, one long wooden stool, aluminium camp-oven and billies under the table. Twisted wire hooks hanging over the soggy ashes of the last fire. The smell of old smoke and ashes.

No one had been here for a long time and there wasn't much food around. A milk-powder tin a third full of mouldy brown rice, some suspicious-looking curry-powder in a coffee jar, two packets of instant soup with the corners chewed by rats, some broken pieces of candle and a thin piece of soap. It didn't look very promising to me, but Uncle Hec seemed to think it was okay. There wasn't even anything to read there.

We tied up the dogs in case they took off after something they were scenting downstream and got a big fire going, which immediately made everything look much better. We ate the rest of the mutton, the last of the second-to-last loaf of bread, half the rice and some mugs of tea. It was still getting dark when I flopped onto a bunk and went to sleep. I thought I heard Uncle Hec get up in the night to deal with a possum in a trap he'd found and set beneath the tree behind the hut, and next thing I knew it was morning and the fire was blazing and the tea-billy was starting to sizzle round the edges.

"Sleep all right?" asked Uncle Hec, poking more wood into the fire.

"Did I ever," I said, sitting up and yawning. "I'm sore all over."

"Not surprised," he said. "You walked right across the Huiarau Range yesterday."

"Is that a long way?"

"It's a bit further than you usually have to walk to get to a hut in here."

"I sure hope so," I said. "I can hardly move."

"Well we don't have to do much today," he said, handing me my mug of tea. "We should be able to get a bit of pork around here, and after a day or two we can take a wander over to the next hut."

"How far's that?"

"About two and a half hours. You can hang round here today and take it easy if you like. I'll just nick out and see if I can knock up an eating-pig for us."

"No you don't," I said. "I'm coming with you."

So after we'd had a feed of bread and rice and sat round for a while, we went up a side creek for a hunt. We'd only been going for a few minutes when we came across a little bush flat freshly turned over by pigs. The dogs shot up into the bush and dragged a little fat boar squealing down into the creek and held it there by an ear each. It was too easy. We carried it out onto the main creek bed and singed it over a driftwood and green manuka fire. That night we cut it up and roasted it in its own fat in the Forestry camp-oven. We ate half of it with a big bundle of watercress. Unfortunately we used up nearly all the rest of the bread.

I was glad we didn't have to walk far that day. I had some blisters on my feet I wasn't mentioning to Uncle Hec and it hurt like anything to walk. I put some paper in my socks when we walked over to the Te Pua hut next day and it wasn't as bad as I thought it was going to be. We climbed up a long ridge, then back down to a big creek on the other side which we followed down to the hut, where there was nothing worth mentioning. The hut itself was much the same as the last one, except that there was no food at all.

We stayed the night at Te Pua, sharpened our knives on a piece of oilstone we found under the steps, and moved on next day across another big ridge to the Tauwharana hut. There was half a five-kilo bag of flour hanging from the rafter and some old yeast in a jar on a shelf, and Uncle Hec showed me how to make a loaf of bread in the camp-oven. You have to keep that yeasty water at just the right temperature and have the fire at the same heat for an hour and a half to get one to turn out right. It was good to know we could actually make our own bread.

Things were looking better in the food department, but by this time I knew I could never find my way out of there on my own. Keeping Uncle Hec in sight through the bush became even more important than finding food. He wasn't my best bet any more, he was my only chance of staying alive.

CHAPTER
FOUR

A TIN OF
PEACHES

After that we walked hundreds of hours through the bush from hut to hut — Otanetea, Tukurua hut, Ngahirimai hut — all the same and all very scrappy as far as supplies went. We weren't eating for the taste of it any more, we were eating for energy to get to the next hut. And what we ate was usually a mixture of what we had left over from the last camp, what we could shoot or catch on the way, and what we found in the next hut when we got there.

Flour, rice and sugar were the main things we liked to find. We had a rice-bag with a mixture of rice from just about every hut, but it still wasn't much. Tea and matches were no trouble — they were left in almost every hut — but condensed milk, sugar and tins of meat or fish were the rarest and best finds. Once I got the hang of it I got to make better loaves of bread than Uncle Hec, so after a few loaves he got to keeping the wood coming while I baked the loaf. It was his way of saying that my loaf was better than his, though he'd never say it right out.

The dogs mostly did okay on the possums they dragged out of banks and clumps, but we had to be aware all the time of what we needed to make up the next couple of feeds. There were a few other drastic changes as well — there was more to it than I'd imagined, living in the bush. At first I was so busy just walking and trying to keep up that I didn't get much chance to look around. In fact it took me a couple of weeks to realise just where we were and what we were doing.

All this bush — there was so much of it. You could stand on a high ridge and as far as you could see in every direction rose other high ridges of bush, disappearing into the distance, split by slips and creeks and bluffs, but always with the bush growing in and on and around everything. There were times when I really didn't think I'd ever see open land again. Sometimes the country we travelled through was so steep and broken up you noticed every flat area, even if it was only big enough to put your foot on. In other places the ridges were long and easy and open under the trees, and the rivers wide and flat, but I soon found out that you never travel far in the Urewera without coming across rough going.

Uncle Hec was good at getting through the bush. The supplejack vines parted in front of him and closed again in front of me in a series of tough tangles. Pigfern up to your chest seemed to lean aside in front of him and stitch itself together behind him so cunningly that I sometimes had to break the stalks to get through, by which time Uncle Hec would be way ahead again. When crossing rivers Uncle Hec would walk straight through at the head of the rapids, propping one leg downstream against the drag of the current. He made it look so easy I was always getting into trouble. Even when I put my foot exactly where his had been I usually stood on a slippery rock. Overbalancing in rivers can make you very bad-tempered.

The result of all this was that I was always hurrying to catch up with Uncle Hec, and whenever I did catch him it was usually only for a few yards before all of a sudden he'd be away ahead again. Then he'd have a spell till I came puffing up, when he'd move off again, making me keep going to stay caught up.

But after a while it became less of a hassle. I wasn't getting blisters and cramps in my leg muscles any more, and I was learning how to weave my way through the ferns and vines and branches.

"If you try to break off every twig and fern that gets in your way," said Uncle Hec one day without looking round, "you'll be worn away long before you've made any impression on the Urewera."

He was right. The bush had us so absolutely outnumbered in every direction you had to have respect for it. No one could live in there without sticking to the rules. No tawa tree was ever going to reach out and steady me when I tripped on one of its roots. No ridge was going to level off any sooner just because I was too tired to climb any higher. No flooded river was going to ease off to let me across. If it wanted to rain, or blow a gale, or freeze or flood or get dark when we were still two hours away from the nearest hut, it certainly didn't take my preferences into account. The bush just stood there, growing and minding its own business.

I know all this is pretty obvious, but some things take a while to sink in when everything's strange and new to you. And there were things in that bush I'm glad I didn't know about at first. Like the time we were walking through a little valley off the Kahikatea Range and the dogs got excited about something up in the bush above us. We hadn't seen much fresh deer-sign around in that area so in case it was a pig we could eat we let them go, and they dived away up into the bush. We waited for a minute or two and then Zag let out his bark when he finds. Next thing they were both bailing hard. Whatever it was hadn't moved, which was a bit unusual.

"I don't know what that'll be," said Uncle Hec, dropping his pack and checking the rifle. "I'd better go up and have a look. You wait here in case it comes this way." And he took off half-running up the side.

I knew he didn't want me to go up there in case it was dangerous, and I don't know what I was supposed to do if anything did come my way, but I let it pass. The dogs were going mad up on the ridge by this time so I jogged out onto the open riverbed where I could see both ways and hear better. Suddenly Willy let out a yelp. He was hurt. Then there was silence.

I was just going to yell out to Uncle Hec when something came crashing down like a falling boulder through a ferny vine-filled gully and out through a stony place to the riverbed where it suddenly stopped, right under the bank I'd just slid down. It was a huge grey boar, like a big piece of an elephant, with pricked-up hairy ears and dark sunken tufts for eyes. Its mouth was frothing and chomping on its big white tusks and its tail was slapping from side to side while it stood there.

If you'd never heard or seen a pig before you'd know this one was definitely dangerous. And there I was standing right out in the open, thirty feet away from it, and I couldn't tell if it had seen me or not. We stood like that forever, then suddenly this great big thing let out a WHOOF and ran downstream, bigger than ever, through the creek with a shower of water and round the corner, heading up into the bush on the other side.

Then Willy and Zag came tearing down after him and that got me moving again. I yelled at them and ran to head them off, and when they hesitated I grabbed them by the scruffs and held them back. Willy had a four-inch rip up his back leg, but it didn't seem to be bothering him too much. Uncle Hec came sliding down.

"Did you get a look at it?" he said.

"Did I! It was standing right there, looking at me."

He hadn't seen it at all. It had broken away before he could get there, but he believed me how big it was when we found its footprints in the sand where it had crossed the creek. The heel of Uncle Hec's No. 9 boot just fitted into the boar's hoofprint. It was a spiritual experience for me, that, the discovery that there were some scary things in this bush.

"No good to us, a thing that size," Uncle Hec said, examining Willy's ripped leg and giving him a slap on the rump. "We don't want any big old boars or twelve-point stags — leave those to the sportsmen. We need meat, and if one of these dogs gets put out of action it could ruin our whole act."

"What do we do if they get a big one bailed up?" I asked.

"Call the dogs off it and if they come, walk away and leave it there. We've got to try and get it through their heads that we don't want boars."

"Could we shoot a big boar like that with the .22?"

"Sure, if you know what you're doing. There's a hollow in the side of a pig's head between its eye and its ear. If you can hit 'em in there at the right angle with the .22 they'll go down all right. Don't you try it, though."

"Even big boars like the one I just saw?"

"The biggest, mate. I'll show you one of these days."

He did, too. Many times. *Crack* — and down they went, except once, but that was a disaster which happened much later.

"I don't know if I ever want to see anything like that again," I said.

"Garn," he said, "in a couple of weeks you'll be going in on pigs like that with your knife," and he reached out to pretend to ruffle my hair, so I ducked and pretended to flatten him with a punch in the ribs and we grabbed our packs and carried on down the valley, keeping the dogs in behind until we were well past where that great big boar had gone up the side.

Half an hour further down the creek we were cutting across a bush flat and the dogs took off and found a big black-and-tan razorback sow. They were out on the river stones where they'd caught her and she was so skinny and putting up such a brave fight that we decided to let her go. We grabbed the dogs and held them off, waiting for the pig to take off into the bush, but she turned and charged us. I had to let Willy go to dodge her, but the dog grabbed her again so Zag had to be released to help keep her still. By this time she had Willy by the skin of his ribs and they were standing there shaking each other.

This time we got the pig down on the ground where Uncle Hec held it while I took the dogs about fifty yards away and grabbed their necks. Then he let go of the pig and shoved it round facing the bush. But it turned straight round and charged him, chasing him over to the bank. He almost made it to the top when he slid back down again, right into the pig. He kicked at its head but it grabbed his boot in its mouth and there he was, hopping around on one leg trying to keep his balance with this big skinny Urewera pig on the end of his other leg.

I released the dogs again but by the time they got to the pig Uncle Hec was on the ground. The dogs flew into the pig and pinned it as it stood astride Uncle Hec, squealing in his face. I was laughing so much I had trouble dragging him clear, but Uncle Hec wasn't amused. He leapt up, grabbed the pig, tipped it over and stuck it before kicking and yelling at the dogs till they settled down again.

"What's so funny?" he said, putting his knife back in its sheath.

"You should have seen it," I told him, "when it had you by the foot and you were hopping round..." I broke up laughing again.

"It wouldn't have looked so funny if it'd had *you* down on your fat bum," he said, examining the marks in the leather of his boot from the pig's teeth. "Anyway, let's get out of this valley before we run into any more of these pigs. They're crazy round here."

≈

We hardly ever stayed more than two or three nights in any hut on the same visit, mainly because it usually only took that long to pick off the animals nearby and clean up most of what we found to eat in the hut. We nearly always got a pig or a bird or some watercress or something to eat between huts. For a while we ate well on grey ducks, which seemed to be everywhere, but then they got scarce and we had a spell on smoked eel from the river.

At the Onepu hut we laid a big bushy manuka tree in a pool with a lump of stinking meat tied in the middle of it, and when we pulled it out and shook it over the stones nine freshwater crayfish fell out. Kura, the Maori call them. They're just like little brown crayfish and steamed in salty water they're delicious, but you'd have to work at it to get enough to live on.

When it rains in the bush there's nothing to say it's not going to keep it up forever, and quite often we had to move on in the wet to find something to eat. Walking in the rain can be not unpleasant once you're properly wet and moving; in fact we did some of our best times between huts and camps in the rain. And we'd arrive at our destination each with a branch broken off a dead tree. By the time I'd broken up the wood for him and got out of my wet clothes Uncle Hec would have a fire going that would roast the rain away from us and our gear, cook our food, dry our rifle and make everything worthwhile. The dogs would sneak in as though we hadn't seen them and lie very still at the side of the fire out of the way, in case someone noticed them and sent them outside.

When the weather was fine we sometimes camped out in the open and built up nice big fires. I'm one of those people who have an annoying attraction for smoke. Whenever I sit by a fire the smoke changes direction so it can blow on me and it's no use changing my position because the smoke always follows me around. I usually spend a lot of time sitting holding my breath with my eyes tight shut and my hand over my mug of tea, waiting for a gust of smoke and heat and ashes to blow past.

There was none of that with Uncle Hec's fires. They were positive, they were alive, they talked to you. He built up a stack of blazing logs that sucked the steam from round your socks and carried the flames and light jumping out through the trees, and the smoke had nowhere to go but upwards. When I used to try and build good fires they never came alive properly until Uncle Hec started mucking around with them.

"There's a knack in it," he'd say, and a few minutes later we'd have to shift everything further back from the heat.

Early afternoon one day we were still twenty minutes from the Pukareao hut when we smelt wood smoke. Someone was around. We climbed onto the bush face opposite the hut and watched. They had no dogs as far as we could see, and we kept ours right beside us. There were two of them, a man and a woman, youngish. Trampers by the look of them and their gear. Their packs were sitting on the ground outside the hut and they were going in and out packing up their stuff. We only had to wait half an hour or so for them to take off in the direction from which we'd come.

I must say it felt a bit strange, sitting there watching other people and knowing we couldn't go up and talk to them without landing in trouble.

"What do we do if we suddenly come across people like that?"

"Play it by ear, I suppose. There's not much anyone can do to us in here anyway."

The trampers hadn't left much food behind them — a packet of instant oxtail soup, half a bottle of tomato sauce and a nearly empty tin of condensed milk. There was a Leon Uris I hadn't read there though — *Trinity*. But we had no candle and I couldn't read at night.

The next morning I was a few minutes walk up the Pukareao stream looking for watercress when suddenly I saw this deer standing among some logs across the river. I ducked round behind some toe-toe and ran back to the hut, where Uncle Hec had just lit the fire. We grabbed the rifle and ran back up to the flat to get there before the deer smelt our smoke. The deer was walking across the stream towards the bush on our side. Uncle Hec leant the rifle across a log and next thing — *crack* — and the deer dropped into the creek right where it was. We went over and bled it. A yearling hind, shot right through the head. He was a good shot, my Uncle Hec.

We dragged the deer back to the hut and skinned it and hung it in a tree. The next day we started on the backsteaks, as many thick juicy steaks as we could eat. They were delicious. We ate all the steaks and chops and made a big camp-oven stew. Uncle Hec poked me in the stomach and tried to put it across that I'd eaten a whole deer practically on my own in four days. I can't help it if I happen to like venison, but I'd had enough of it by the time we left.

From Pukareao we travelled on to Totaepukepuke hut, and then on to the Poplars in the Horomanga Valley. Uncle Hec had a few rules about the huts but sometimes I thought he went a bit far with them. We never skinned a hut right out of food, even if we only left a brew of tea there, and we had to leave a good heap of wood at every hut we used, to make everything nice and tidy "for the next man". That next man burnt a whole lot more of our firewood than we burnt of his, that's all I can say.

Mangapouri hut . . . Opaheru . . . Mangarawhia hut — pretty soon we had the best eating utensils you could find anywhere. It was just a matter of swapping something of yours for a better one whenever you found it. We used plastic mugs and plates because they were lighter and made less noise than tin ones.

The Bullring hut . . . Mangakahika hut . . . Central Waiau . . . Te Waiotukapati. We found plenty of clothes in the huts — shirts, socks, coats, even pants. Nothing was in pairs or fitted us properly, but we could keep ourselves clothed, which was the main thing.

Boots were another thing. Our feet were hardly ever dry and I'd had my boots for nearly a year. We knew they were going to pack it in and they did — in a side-creek of the Waikare River. The sole of my right boot came right away from the upper. We flapped around and perched ourselves on a low ridge and watched the main track to the Waikare hut. We were hoping to find something, but towards evening a bunch of trampers came up the track. We heard one of the women laughing minutes before they came in sight. Two men and two women, obviously intending to stay the night in the Waikare hut.

That was the end of any idea of fixing my boot that night, and we couldn't get far with it as it was. We had to adapt, so we sidled around in the bush to where we could see the hut. Four pairs of boots were propped upside-down against the steps to drain — and the people were all inside, eating and talking and laughing. So I snuck round and exchanged my boots for the nearest-sized pair and crept away in my socks before someone came out and saw me.

We would have liked to wait around to see what happened when they discovered the boot-switch, but it was getting dark and we had to go for it to get a camping place under an overhang we'd used once before. My new boots were so good to walk in that I felt a bit remorseful about taking them. I hope they made it out to the road with my old boots, whoever they were.

Parahaki hut . . . Whakataka hut . . . Manuoha. It was only when we were going round some of the huts for the second or third time that I started to learn the actual lay of the land. The whole of the Uruwera has two main ranges, the Huiarau and the Ikawhenua, with the Whakatane River valley between them. If you could keep your position related to some point on one of those ranges you could usually tell which valley you were in. And if the water was running the right way you were probably in the right creek or river. It was very hit and miss and we spent a lot of time uncertain exactly where we were. Most of the trouble was not being able to see out through the bush; you get a lot of mist in the Urewera, too.

I got to studying the bits of maps we found in various huts and gradually built up an understanding of the way the ridges and rivers ran. Everything was right there on the maps. In the Upper Whirinaki hut one night I tried to point out something I'd found on a map to Uncle Hec, and I suddenly realised he didn't know what I was talking about. Uncle Hec couldn't even read a map.

"You can't even read a map," I accused him. "Can you!"

"Never needed to," he said.

"But that's why we have to guess where we *are* half the time," I said. "That's what maps are for, so you can tell exactly where you are. Don't you realise that?"

"I usually get there," he said.

He was impossible — too old-fashioned. I decided to take over some of our navigation and it wasn't long before I knew more about some of the areas than Uncle Hec. I also knew enough not to let him know it. He fancies himself in the bush, Uncle Hec, but there were two places where we'd walked for hours up gorgy creeks when a track had been benched into the face since he'd known it in the old days.

None of the smaller creeks had names on the maps so we usually had to refer to them by something that happened there. So we had an Earache Creek, Cast-antler Creek, Milkpowder-tin Creek, Always-raining Creek, Cowbones Creek — names like that. At Deep Creek, we had to follow the right bank for more than an hour to find a place to get across; at Cathedral Creek we camped among a stand of huge totara trees, rising straight out of the ground like big pillars.

How Log-jamb Creek got its name was a bit scary. We'd slept beside this creek, under a sheet of black polythene we'd found in one of the huts. It had been raining and drizzling on and off for a couple of days and the main river was up about a metre. We kept a fire going with lumps of shattered rata and just after dawn I went over to the creek to get a billy of water and noticed that it had almost stopped flowing altogether. I thought this was a bit strange and told Uncle Hec, "The creek's stopped flowing and the river's flooded."

"What?" He hurried over to see for himself, then rushed back to the camp and started pulling down the polythene.

"Get packed up and get the hell out of here," he said urgently.

"What's the hurry?" I said, stuffing things into my pack.

"A slip's come down in the night and blocked off the creek," he said. "The water builds up behind 'em and when they go they can be like a dirty great tidal wave."

We went straight up onto a small terrace on the ridge above and got a new fire going with burning sticks from the old one. Then we set up our shelter and sat there, about 300 feet above the creek.

"You've got to watch out for this sort of thing," Uncle Hec said. "I've seen one of those slip dams bury a hut under thirty metres of shingle when it — listen!"

And we could hear it coming with a rumbling grinding noise. A big slow wave of water and logs and branches, an enormous brown stew, surged around the corner of the creek from where we were, smashing flat and breaking off the bush at the sides and shaking and bruising the bark off the big trees. It was like a tidal wave, tearing past us like a giant train through the bush and fading off down the valley. Then there was only the rain hissing onto the leaves all around us.

We looked at each other but didn't say anything. There was only one thing to say and we both knew it. We'd beaten that destruction by under an hour.

Next morning on our way out we went down and looked at the flat where we'd camped. A two-metre wall of water and mud and broken timber had swept right through it, leaving some places ankle-deep in sloppy silt and others washed away completely. The whole creek had been altered forever in that one rush of water, and only Uncle Hec and I in the whole world knew what the name of Log-jamb Creek really meant.

Another place we named was Mossy Rocks — and that was a close shave, too. We were crossing this gorgy rocky place on a big rimu log about fifteen feet above the creek. The dogs were barking on something up around the corner and we were in a hurry to catch up and see what they had.

We weren't being careful enough. I was in front and I stood on a slippery part of the log. My foot shot out from under me and Uncle Hec grabbed my pack to try and steady me. We almost made it, but ever so slowly we both fell off the log and down through the air, crashing down onto some mossy rocks at the edge of the creek. Like when a stone explodes in the fire and a splinter snicks past your eye, your mind concentrates for a flash on how very far from any outside help you are if you get hurt.

We lay there for a moment, wondering how seriously hurt we were. We stood up slowly and looked at each other. No broken arms or legs, not even a bruise or scratch that we could see. Uncle Hec picked the rifle up out of the water. There was a dent bruised into the wood on the forestock. We shook the water out of it and had a couple of shots each at stones in a bank. It was okay.

"There was someone in our corner that time," said Uncle Hec, looking up at the log we'd just fallen off.

Our camps had to have names, too. There was Shag-rookery Camp, Wet-bread Cliffs, Stag-wallow Saddle, Lost-soap Pool, Duck-egg Flats, Kaka Ridge, Sparrowhawk Bend — in fact if there'd been anyone around to hear us talking they wouldn't have known where we were talking about.

One night we camped at the Kanohirua hut on the Maungapohatu Track, and Uncle Hec went down to the Ruatahuna Settlement to try and contact a friend of his called Russ. He was away all night and as soon as he got back to the hut next day we had to go up to the Huiarau road to pick up a beautiful big load of food from the mysterious Russ's wife.

I was a bit hacked-off with Uncle Hec because he'd promised to ask if they had any spare books and he'd forgotten. He had some interesting news, though. We'd been in the newspapers. He had a newspaper cutting about us, so I made him stop on the track while I read it.

It said that Hector William Faulkner, aged fifty-three years, and his nephew, Richard Morehu Baker, a part-Maori aged thirteen, had disappeared from the Faulkners' Apopo farm over three months before. They were believed to be somewhere in the Urewera Country and fears were held for their safety. Although Hector Faulkner was known to be an experienced bushman, his relatives were concerned about his state of mind since the recent loss of his wife. The Forest Service and National Park Rangers had been alerted to keep a lookout for the pair, and anyone sighting them should inform the nearest ranger or police station immediately.

"They reckon it's been over the radio a few times too," said Uncle Hec. "They seem to be making a hell of a fuss about it."

"Do you think they'll come looking for us?" I said.

"Not seriously," he said. "There's too much bush for us to hide ourselves in. My guess is that they'll wait for us to crack up and go out and give ourselves up."

"That'll be the day."

"They probably think we won't be able to handle the winter. It gets a bit heavy in here some years."

"We can hold out through the winter, can't we?"

"Sure we can. They won't get us that way, but we'd better try and avoid being spotted by anyone in case they send a search party after us. They're doing some pretty weird things out there these days. I sure wouldn't have thought they'd have been all that interested in us."

Not long after that (five days), we were in the Tawhiwhi hut on the Whakatane River. Mid-morning it was, and suddenly there was a rifle shot just down the end of the flat. We didn't wait to tidy up for the next man, not that time. Luckily we were getting ready to leave for the Takurua at the time and our packs were sitting on the floor of the hut. We threw everything of ours we could see into the packs, untied the dogs, and took off quietly into the bush behind the hut. We must have been only just out of sight when we heard someone shout, "Hey, Mike! You there, mate?"

We climbed straight up the ridge behind the hut. Fortunately the night was fine and still, so we camped by a stag-wallow on a saddle high on the Te Wharau Ridge. That was where we discovered we'd left our tea-billy behind at the Tawhiwhi hut, and we had to boil water in our mugs against the embers of the fire to make a brew.

We arrived at the Otanetea hut the next day and saw our new brew-billy sitting on the table. It was a tin of golden peaches, a large one. It was sitting on a note that said, FOR JOAN AND REG, COMPLIMENTS OF RAY AND DAVID.

We ate the peaches and later on, when we'd had something more to eat, we made holes in the peach tin with a nail worked out of the wall of the hut and put a wire handle in it. Just right for two mugs of tea.

If we'd known then some of the things that were going to happen to us while that peach tin was our brew-billy we mightn't have got quite so much fun out of swapping a third of a jar of expired yeast for it on the note on the table of the Otanetea hut.

CHAPTER

FIVE

BROKEN-FOOT
CAMP

On our next trip round the huts, about two weeks later, we'd left the right branch of the Manuoha Creek one day, heading for the Mangawhero Forks, and on a narrow track down a ridge we ran into two men and two women coming the other way. Even the dogs were taken by surprise. The only thing to do was stop and talk — we couldn't walk *through* them. It was the first other people I'd been this close to since Aunty Bella's funeral. My heart was thumping.

"Hello there," someone said.

"G'day," said Uncle Hec. "Where are you lot heading?"

"We're on our way out to the road from — hey! You're not the ones they're looking for, are you?"

"What do you mean looking for?" said Uncle Hec.

"Everyone's been asked to keep a lookout for a middle-aged man and a young Maori boy. They've been missing in the bush for over three months."

"No kidding," said Uncle Hec.

"Sure, haven't you heard about it?"

"Couldn't be us, mate. We've only come in here for the weekend. Hunting."

One of the women caught me sneaking a look at the watch to see what day of the week it was. Thursday.

"Well if you do see anyone like that, tell them they're supposed to report to the nearest police station urgently."

"Okay, we'll do that," said Uncle Hec, moving past them. "Have a nice walk."

"Thanks, the same to you."

And we were away from them along the track. We didn't stop or say anything until we'd reached the creek at the bottom of the ridge.

"Do you think they knew it was us?" I asked after we'd dropped our packs and had the billy hanging in the fire.

"For sure," said Uncle Hec. "They'd have to be pretty dumb not to. They'll go straight out and tell the police they saw us."

"What would the police want us for?"

"It's *me* they want."

"Why?"

"Taking you off into the bush, I suppose."

"But there's no law against that, is there?"

"If there's not they'll probably make one," he said. "They're doing some pretty strange things out there these days."

"Why can't they just leave us alone?" I said. "It's not fair."

"If you're looking for a fair deal, forget it," said Uncle Hec. "You'd only ever run into one of those by accident."

Knowing that those trampers would probably report seeing us, and where, we climbed onto the main ridge and dropped over into the Pukareao Stream and stayed the night in the Pukareao hut. And the next day on our way to Ngahirimai we walked straight into two men with rifles in the Whakatane River. We walked right up to them and past them.

"G'day," said one of them.

"G'day," said Uncle Hec without stopping.

And when we were twenty or so yards past them one of them called out, "Hey!"

We stopped and looked back.

"You two are supposed to report to the nearest police station urgently."

"Yeah," said Uncle Hec. "We already got the message."

And we walked on away from them.

"We'd better get out of this area," said Uncle Hec. "It's crawling with other people around here."

So we climbed another long ridge, over the Te Mauia Range and down the other side to a big creek, where we caught a skinny pig and camped on a sandy river-beach. From there we crossed the Kairaka Range and picked up a stash of food we had hidden near the Te Pua hut. Another day's walking brought us to a jumble of short steep ridges and waterfally creeks. There was plenty of deer- and pig-sign around and we caught a good pig and camped where the creek we were following opened out into a fairly wide area of shingle and bush-flats. It was the hardest, longest walk we'd done for a long time.

"We might get left alone here for a bit," said Uncle Hec. "But we'll still have to keep out of sight of the choppers. I wouldn't be surprised if they've been told to keep a watch out for us."

"Where are we, anyway?" I said.

"Right in the guts of it," he said.

And it was easy to believe him. The bush here was steeper and more primitive-looking than over in the Whakatane Valley. The creeks were narrower and steeper and the pigs skinnier and nastier — they chased the dogs. Harder sort of country — even the same ferns seemed coarser and scratchier here.

As far as I could figure out from the torn scrap of map I had of the area, we were in a side-creek in the headwaters of the Ruakituri River. Right, as Uncle Hec said, in the guts of it. Strange territory, lost among more strange territory. When it rained the day after we got there even the downpour seemed wetter than usual, but we soon had a worse problem than just getting wet — when we were setting up our camp a certain uncle pulled a big rock out of the bank to shield one side of the fireplace, and it fell onto his boot against another rock and broke a bone in his foot.

In an hour we knew he couldn't walk, and it was going to be a long time before he was going to get a boot on that foot again. We were stuck right there until his foot mended, and boy, he didn't like the idea of *that* very much.

When the rain stopped we built a really good camp in a grove of trees back from the stream. We cut poles with the slasher-head we'd found on a track over in the Whakatane, and tied them between the trees with vines to make punga walls and bunks. We used punga-fronds a foot thick over a sheet of black polythene for thatching, tied down with thin poles. And we built a big fireplace between Uncle Hec's big rock and the bank, a few feet from the doorway.

We'd bound up his broken foot with shirtsleeves and he could hobble around with a stick, tying knots and giving bad-tempered orders — but that was about all. I was going to have to do all the hunting till his foot mended, however long that was going to take. We had to have meat or our other food would be gone in a few days. I was going to be busy.

We were out of meat by the time I went for my first hunt and I *had* to get something. The dogs got interested in the wind from a narrow side-creek about twenty minutes upstream from our camp, and when I investigated I found a small mob of goats on a rocky slip down near the creek. There were six of them. I shot a young nanny goat through the neck and the others all ran into the bush. The dogs scrambled up through the jumbled rocks and bailed up a billygoat on top of a boulder as big as a Forestry hut. He was a white one with a long yellow beard and mane, and his horns curled out from his head in thick twists of bone. And he really stank. He fought the dogs off for about ten minutes — no way were they getting up on his rock if he had any say in it. He shunted them off one after the other as they tried to claw their way up the slope of the boulder to get at him. And he was still looking for more. A brave goat, that one.

I called the dogs off and we left him there in charge of his boulder. I then carried the goat I'd shot back to camp. If it was as easy as this to get meat around here . . . but it wasn't.

"Where'd you get this?" said Uncle Hec, flopping the dead goat from side to side.

"Second creek on the right up the left fork. Brave Goat Creek."

"Many there?"

"Five left out of the mob I saw, and another billygoat. There could be more there — I only got two minutes up the creek."

"Could come in handy."

He never asked me how it got to be called Brave Goat Creek — we just always called it Brave Goat Creek after that. Not bad meat, goat, but I always preferred mutton or pork or venison.

The next time I went out I got right up into the head of a creek before the dogs got onto a mean little boar that was only just worth eating. It gave Willy a rip up the shoulder and it took me three and a half hours to get it back to the camp.

Meantime Uncle Hec hobbled around with his stick, throwing every bit of firewood he could reach into a huge heap beside the camp. His foot looked pretty painful to me but he never said much about it. He hated having anything wrong with him, Uncle Hec.

Next time I left him soaking his foot in the edge of the creek and went downstream where I walked all day without even seeing any fresh sign. The game that had been so plentiful when we had arrived had moved away. I got back to camp an hour or so after dark, wet and miserable with rain and failure. The dogs hadn't had a run all day.

But Uncle Hec was looking smug about something and I didn't find out what it was until he raked a big rainbow trout, baked in clay, out of the embers of the fire. He'd hobbled over to the big pool at the forks, about 150 metres, and caught it with a cricket on a hook and reel of nylon we had with our gear. It must have been tricky getting it landed without breaking the nylon because you usually had to run up and down among the stones, following the trout till it tired and you could ease it into the shallows. It must have been quite a performance, the way Uncle Hec was fixed for running, but he never said anything about it. The trout was delicious, though, stuffed with watercress and wineberry. In fact I could have eaten the whole thing on my own if I'd had a chance.

The next day I climbed up onto the ridge at the head of Broken-foot Creek — nothing. It was getting dark and I was half an hour from the camp, empty-handed, and ready to give up when the dogs found something under a branchy log lying head-down the creek bank. There was an animal under there, probably a possum, but it might be a duck or something. I climbed up, pulled a shattered branch away, and Willy dived in. Something black shot out behind me and Zag grabbed it and shook it once before I got it off him. It was a big dark-brown kiwi with a broken neck.

I'd never seen a kiwi close up before. This one was about the same size as an ordinary rooster, with thick brown legs, long thin beak and ferrety little eyes. It had stumps of wings and hairyish speckled feathers, and it felt as if I was holding something prehistoric in my hands. There seemed to be plenty of meat on it so I carried it back to camp. By the time I got it there my hands were cramped with the weight of it.

"Never eaten one meself," said Uncle Hec, flopping the dead kiwi around in the firelight. "You game to give it a go?"

"It's the only meat we've got," I said.

We took the ferny-feathered skin off the dark red flesh and fried it in pieces in the camp-oven we'd carried all the way from Te Pua. Then we worked it up into a kind of casserole with some onion and other stuff we had, but no matter how long we cooked it, it was still like chewing musty fishy rubber.

"You can leave the next one of *them* where you find it," said Uncle Hec, throwing a piece back into the camp oven.

I had to agree with him, and so did the dogs, but it filled a gap till I got a big pig not far from the camp next day.

I managed to keep up with it for the next three weeks. One night it was a big eel I kicked up out of the shallows when I was almost back to the camp with nothing. Another time the dogs grabbed a paradise duck in some long grass. Then we'd catch a pig and have a few days' rest from hunting.

We got lucky too. One day I was having a rake with the dogs through a place I called White-sow Creek, where I'd picked up one or two feeds. Towards the head of the creek the dogs disappeared, so I carried on up, listening for them. Suddenly a red-brown smudge ran through scattered trees and stopped on a little slip, looking back at me. A deer, about forty metres away. I tried to get a bead on its neck but couldn't hold the rifle steady. Shooting at real deer can make you nervous.

The deer turned its head away to move again, so I took wild aim and fired. I knew I'd hit it somewhere by the way it bucked a bit as it jumped out of sight, so I ran round to where it had been standing and started following its marks around the game-trail looking for blood. Then Willy and Zag shot straight past me. There was a single bark in the creek bed 100 metres ahead, and when I got there the dogs were panting around at the foot of the bank beside my deer, dripping and wagging as though they'd done it all by themselves. I'd hit it through the chest — a lung-shot. It was a four-point stag. A big one.

After I'd gutted it I found I could just get it onto my back. I had about an hour to walk down White-sow Creek and then an hour and a half up to the camp with the back legs over my shoulders, the blood dripping down my leg-backs, the deer-smell, the dogs, and the rifle slung across — I was right into the spirit of being a hunter that day, bringing home the meat.

By the time I reached the main creek I'd had to cut the head off because it kept tripping me up. The bones were digging into my shoulders and back and the rifle was banging on my head or knee or elbow — I needed both hands to keep the deer balanced. I fell over a few times and had to have a number of rests, but I was determined to walk into camp with that deer on my back.

I was so tired by the time I saw Uncle Hec's big fire shining in the trees up at the next bend that I had to lean my load on a log and have a little cry about Aunty Bella. After I had staggered into camp Uncle Hec took over the deer and skinned it in the firelight, while I thankfully drank a full billy of tea. There was resting and feasting at Broken-foot for a good spell after that.

After a few days, and while we still had a bit of meat in the camp, I walked over to the Te Panaa hut to look for food. I got back to Broken-foot next night with a big load of flour and quite a bit of other stuff — candles, two magazines, a sheet of plastic, some wire and a tin for a new billy, for watercress because of some boils we were getting on us.

It was a long walk, but it stopped Uncle Hec getting so worried every time I went somewhere on my own. He used to say it was because he didn't like not having the rifle around him in the bush.

I was learning a few things from living in the bush. One of them was that there's a big difference between hunting for fun and having to do it to eat. Hunting had become like work that had to be done. Sneaking through the bush, always looking for something to kill and eat. Needing the meat. There was something savage about it, something kind of primitive.

"Do you think it's good for anyone to kill things all the time, Uncle Hec?"

"What sort of things?"

"Animals. Pigs, deer, fish. Stuff like that."

"Long as y' don't start enjoying cutting throats there's nothin' t' worry about."

No fear of that with me. And there were always the nice things, like the birds. I always liked birds and I'd got to know most of them in the Urewera. The shining cuckoo, arriving each year from across the world to lead the dawn chorus in the Urewera — how about that? And the silly cheeky old weka, spearing around in the undergrowth. The soft grey bush robin, and the pretty moppy little fantail. Then there was the beautifully dressed green-and-white bush pigeon, and the acrobatic kaka showing off in the high beeches. The fluffy morepork owl, ruru, hooting to his mates all night across the gully, and the dangerous diving sparrowhawk, hurtling through the tree-tops. The green little bellbird with the melodious voice, and the blue-black tui in the yellow kowhai tree. The wind-up walk of the pukeko, the fearless blue mountain duck bobbing through the rapids, and the hovering harrier hawk, looking for a mouse or a frog or something dead. There was the bushman's friend, the miromiro I think he was, the shape and colour of a kid's drawing, and the jagged shag, sitting on a stick in the river with a bellyful of trout fingerlings, holding his wings out to dry so he can lift off. The white-faced heron, pale and delicate and shy, minding his own business out there along the edge of the river.

There were more birds than that, but you mightn't like them as much as I do. In fact I spent a lot of hours watching birds when I suppose I should have been hunting. One of my games was pretending to be a wildlife photographer commissioned to get shots of birds in their natural habitat for a big nature magazine — *National Geographic*, perhaps. And if my chunk of wood had been a camera I'd have taken some interesting photos. It was more like practice really, in case I decided to take it up as a career, or something.

A funny thing happened about that. One day I was creeping after a kaka I'd seen from the camp, trying to get a shot of its orange underwings, using the rifle as a camera. Uncle Hec, dragging a big dead tawa branch, spotted me sneaking along.

"What are you up to?" he said.

"I was just trying to sneak up on that kaka."

"What for? You don't want to eat them. There's not enough on one to fill the holes in your teeth."

"I was trying to see if I could get a photograph of it, if I had a camera," I confessed.

He squatted down against a tree and started breaking up a stick of wood.

"Is that what you want to get into?" he asked.

"Wouldn't mind," I said. "What's wrong with that? I know a lot about birds. I watch them all the time. I bet I know more about them than you do."

"Photographing 'em might turn out to be a bit trickier than just looking at 'em," he said.

"I can learn photography," I told him. "I've read a bit about it. Enough to know the kind of camera and lenses you need. They might even have better gear out by now, but I know I can suss it out pretty quick."

"All you'd have left to do after that is suss out how to get close enough to the birds."

"I already know that," I said. "I spend hours just watching . . ."

Uncle Hec flicked the end of his stick at me and it hit me in the chest. "I mean close," he said. "You don't understand the first thing about birds. You're going the wrong way about it for a start."

"I suppose you know all there is to know about them," I said, getting ready to dodge a flattening. I reckoned I could outrun him these days, especially with him having a lame foot.

"Birds are some of the hardest things to sneak up on you'll ever find," he went on. "Even for another bird. And here you are creeping along staring at them like a hungry cat." He shook his head at the sheer stupidity of it.

"What am I supposed to do then?"

"Well look at it this way. A bird'll sit on a sheep's back, it'll feed round a horse's feet — it'll even sit in a crocodile's mouth and pick his teeth — but the same bird won't come within a stag's roar of a human being. What do you reckon causes that?"

"Don't know," I said.

"It's because human beings are so unpredictable," he said. "One of the sheep isn't going to leap up and chuck a stone all of a sudden. They're indifferent to the birds. That's your clue.

"Birds are territorial, mostly, and the best way to get near 'em is to move into their territory and ignore them. You can keep an eye on 'em without staring at 'em. You don't want to stay too still, either. Things waiting in ambush do that. You just move quietly around minding your own business. Like a sheep. Then it's a matter of your own patience."

"Patience?"

"Yeah. You might have to wait an hour or more for the bird life in a place to settle down, once you disturb it, and not many people like to stick around that long. Especially young blokes." He looked at me.

"It's not like waiting to me," I told him.

He shrugged and stood up. "I won't stop you," he said. "Get into it if you want to. You're not going to be in here all your life."

He grabbed the end of his tawa branch and started limping down the creek bed with it towards the camp. I picked up some lighting-sticks and followed him.

"Where did you learn about birds, Uncle Hec?"

"Mostly from an old aboriginal lady I was bushed with once up in Arnhem Land."

"An old lady? What were you doing there?"

"Hunting."

"Hunting what?"

"Snakes, grubs, lizards, birds — anything we could get to eat. The Mornington Islanders had stolen our canoe and all our gear and a load of salted dugong meat. We were cut off by the wet season and all we had was a knife and a burning gum-branch."

"How long did you do that for?"

"About eight weeks. We crossed the Roper River on a log and made it out to the Gulf in the finish and got to a place called Borroloola on the MacArthur River. I got through to Darwin after that and waited out the wet."

"What happened to the old lady?"

"She went back to her tribe on the Limmin River, but I reckon I'd have been dingo meat if it hadn't been for her. I've been in the bush with a few people, but that old abo lady could run rings around anyone else I ever seen."

"How?"

"She just moved so good through the bush she never hassled an ant. She could tell you by the state of the insects what birds were

TOP / Julian Dennison as Ricky.   BOTTOM / Aunt Bella (Rima Te Wiata) sings Ricky's birthday song.

Ricky (Julian Dennison) goes head to head with Hec (Sam Neill) in the bush.

Julian Dennison as Ricky and Sam Neill as Uncle Hec.

Taika Waititi directs the hunters.

Hec and Ricky at Psycho Sam's.

Sam Neill as Uncle Hec and Julian Dennison as Ricky.

Rhys Darby as Psycho Sam.

Tioreore Ngatai-Melbourne as Kahu.

likely to be around, and she could tell by the birds what animals were in their area. She could tell by the mud crabs just where to wait for a barramundi with a burnt sharpened stick. The birds used to carry on as though she wasn't there, and when I'd sneak up behind her they'd start squeaking and flying around as though someone had fired a couple of shots. When we were looking for tucker I had to stay so far behind her I could hardly keep her in sight — I was so clumsy compared with her. I'm not bad in the scrub myself, but the only use I was to her was carrying the fire-stick and helping her roll logs over to get at the grubs."

We walked on for a bit and then he said, "I'd have died on my own. There's no one can sneak like an abo."

"Must have been pretty tough going," I said.

We'd come out on the flat near the camp by this time and he stopped and looked round at me.

"It was no tougher than this."

Uncle Hec had said one of those things I couldn't forget. "*There's no one can sneak like an abo.*" And every time it came into my mind I couldn't help imagining this old black lady taking Uncle Hec out into the desert, years ago in another land, and giving him a message about birds to pass on years later to young black Ricky Baker in the Urewera bush. I felt kind of grateful to her from a long way off. Maybe she was an ancestor of mine or something, or maybe I needed something to fill the gaps of not having much to do with other people. Whatever it was that old lady, the Bird-lady, was with me in the bush whenever I thought about her after that. I even sneaked different, as though she was watching to see if I did it right. She taught me to *like* the vines and roots and bluffs and boulders that got in my way, and suddenly they'd be behind me and nice to have known you. You walk lighter on the land when you like the land you walk on, and you can see your way through a tangle of vines or a heap of rocks or a tricky river before you even reach them. Distance becomes a different thing, too. And time. It alters your pace, to do it right. You move slower but you get there sooner, and quieter, and more convinced than last time that in a mysterious kind of way it's all one big living thing. I had a whole new relationship with the birds to explore, too, and I could get into their scenes real easy once I got used to it. Uncle Hec was right. There's no one can sneak like an abo.

The night after I got back from Te Panaa hut with the load of flour and stuff we had the first heavy frost of the winter. Keeping warm became very important, so we improved our little whare to make it more rain- and wind-proof, made a goatskin door laced onto a framework of wineberry sticks, built up round our fireplace with flat rocks, doubled the depth of crown fern on our bunks and tied extra poles along the roof to hold down the polythene and thatching. It ended up real cosy, especially when the light and heat from the fire reflected right into the hut at night.

The dogs were snug too. Zag had a bunk under the roots of an upturned rimu, and Willy had a speargrass nest under the bank near the fireplace. They were doing fine on the biggest blackest possums Uncle Hec had seen for years.

"There's an unusually good colony of possums round here," he said half a dozen times.

One real cold morning it was just getting daylight and I was lighting the fire when I heard something that sent me ducking in to wake Uncle Hec up.

"Wake up," I said, giving him a shake.

"What's up?" he said, sitting up in his sleeping-bag.

"The stags are roaring," I said. "Listen."

We went outside. A distant moan came wafting down from high on the range at the head of the valley, to be followed by a loud bellowing from up behind the camp. There was another roar from further away, and then silence, expect for the birds.

"They're roaring all right," he said. "We'll have to be extra careful for the next few weeks. The Urewera will be crawling with trophy-hunters — they go everywhere. The choppers'll be busy too. You'd better take the slasher and see how many trees you can drop across that old helicopter pad you found the other day."

So we lit no fires in the daytime and listened and watched for signs of other people. It was an extra worry when I was away scrounging for food, and every time I got back to camp it was a relief to find out that Uncle Hec hadn't had a visit from anyone while I was away. We were very vulnerable just then, with Uncle Hec's foot, and I could tell he was worried about it by his bad temper. I heard two shots one day from way over on the next watershed, and I found gumboot marks crossing our creek two hours downstream from the camp, but nothing worth mentioning to Uncle Hec.

The stags roared around there for four weeks, morning and evening mostly. The big old one high up in the beech country would moan two or three times, then the noisy one on Pigeon Ridge would bellow like a calf, and when he'd had his say the one we called Hookgrass Harry would bellow and bark and grunt in several bursts. He was on a swampy bend in the heads of the little creek opposite the camp, about a quarter of a mile away. Those were the regulars but Uncle Hec said he'd identified twenty-six different stags he'd heard from the camp during the roar. I wondered where they all disappeared to when I was out hunting.

One afternoon at the height of the roar I tied up the dogs and climbed up to see how close to Hookgrass Harry I could sneak. For a start I just headed up in his general direction, and I'd climbed right past him when he let out a roar about fifty yards away. I went prickly with fright. Even the Bird-lady froze. No idea it was going to be *that* loud. I stood there with a bit more than half my attention on a tree I could get up quick, and then he roared again — a rattling rasping bellow that could only come out of something real dangerous, and big.

I knew not be scared, but I still was. I sneaked slowly round to where the noise was coming from. The wind was gusty and blowing everywhere at once, so with a bit of luck it might scent me and run away. It roared again and I skipped a bit closer. The Bird-lady seemed to have stayed back by the leaning tree. Again it roared and I made about twenty yards towards it. I heard something crashing, like gorillas. I moved up behind another tree in a gust of wind and then I saw him.

He was an eight-pointer stag, walking up and down a ten-yard flat place, stopping every now and then to roar again, or rip his antlers through a tanekaha bush that was hanging in shreds of stripped bark and broken branches. It was the biggest deer I'd seen, and I could see why Uncle Hec had said, "Don't try it with the .22, you'll only tickle him."

He had a dark shaggy mane of hair round his neck and a big yellow ring round his rump. The rest of him was thick greyish hair apart from his belly, which was black like his legs. His antlers were brown from tanekaha bark and shining white at the tips. He roared again and gave four or five huge grunts.

I don't know how long I stood there looking at him, perhaps ten minutes, when I turned back from listening to another stag roar further round the face and found that Hookgrass Harry was looking straight at me. He'd seen my head move. It was a nasty moment, that. I've never been looked at so hard by anything in my life, except maybe Uncle Hec when he was getting ready to flatten me. But this was different — a wild animal that roared like a dragon and ripped things to bits with its antlers. I got ready to fire a shot to try and frighten it away, but the stag moved first. He gave a grunt and leapt away, down and across through the bush and he was gone.

I stood there wondering about it. What would a twelve-pointer be like to come across in the roar. Pretty impressive, I imagined. But when I did see one later on the Pohukura Ridge my imaginings were nothing like it. He's a mighty animal, the red stag. You had to have respect for him.

Anyway, the wind had been getting more gusty for an hour or so, and as I made my way back down through the bush it started getting very strong. By the time I got to camp Uncle Hec was hopping around tying down the roof, and the trees were thrashing about in the sudden gusts as though they were throwing fits.

I thought it was going to be a bit of fun at first, but this wasn't any ordinary wind; it was Urewera wind. A roaring, shunting gale developed, broken up by the bush and ridges into aimless buffeting blasts that hit you from any old direction. I realised it was getting serious when the whole fire suddenly blew out of the fireplace with a swirl of ashes and embers and burning bits of wood, streaming sparks and smoke out across the flat, while we stood a few yards away and watched it with no more than a bit of disturbed air blowing around us at the time.

We staggered round with logs from the creek bed to lay on our roof, which was going to lift off and blow away at any moment, groping our way through the wind and stopping and hanging on in the gusts. Every now and then we'd be caught in a driven rain of spray whipped up off the surface of the creek. The whole bush-face opposite the camp was writhing.

When we'd done everything we could to hold the roof on and put rocks on everything that hadn't already blown away, we went inside and sat on our bunks, listening to the power and destruction of it. A big tree came crashing down in the bush across from the camp — one of the dead ratas. The rising roar of the storm tore at the bush until all we could do was to sit in our flimsy lifting whare and grin when we survived another big one.

The wind left our ragged-out valley just before dark that night, to be followed by a thick layer of blue cloud and heavy rain before we could even get the fire going. Urewera rain, it doesn't fall in drops like ordinary rain; it starts like a bucketful of marbles being tipped out on the roof and then it's a continuous stream of white lines, hissing and splashing into the bush, beating everything flat and keeping it there, bouncing spray off every surface.

By dark our creek was up a foot, and by morning — it was still raining — it was more than two metres above normal. We could hear the rocks and logs booming and rumbling down through the heaving brown torrent that had once been our little creek. The rain had its own cold little wind with it which swept the spattering rain through the gaps round the door of our whare, so the only dryish place was in our sleeping-bags on our bunks. We just stayed in bed until the rain eased off into ordinary showers, a couple of hours after daylight. Then we started a tiny fire with a candle-stub, and built it up into a real big one with the aid of man-sized logs brought out of the bush by Uncle Hec on his one leg. Soon everything was steaming and drying out and looking much better with mugs of tea made with dirty water and fresh damper, and the last of the pork and a billy of watercress. What good stuff fire is!

We kept the fire going all that night because it was freezing. Next day we had a frost followed by an overcast sky. The creek was so flooded that you couldn't go anywhere except straight up behind the camp, and it was never any good up there. All we could do was keep the fire going and try to eat as little as possible. The next day was fine but freezing. The creek had gone nearly back to normal, leaving everything changed and swept clean with logs and driftwood piled up in different places and the creek bed itself on a new course across the shingle flats.

I made a quick trip over to the Tataweka hut to try for supplies, and I found that the chopper I'd heard just before I got there had dropped off a fantastic load of stuff — probably for a team of track-cutters. The first thing I did was punch holes in a tin of condensed milk and drink the lot. Then I loaded Uncle Heck's pack with milk, sugar, flour, butter, two loaves of fresh bread, a cabbage, two books and a stretch bandage out of the first-aid box. It was a big load and there was still plenty left. Those Forestry blokes certainly looked after themselves.

I stashed a few tins of peas and cheese and milk under a tawa down the flat from the hut and then had another poke through to see if there was anything I ought to add to my load. But the sound of a chopper sent me off down the track in a hurry. Just as well, too, because that load almost did for me, getting it back to Broken-foot.

Uncle Hec was pleased to see me and my big load of goodies. "You needn't have brought all that," he said. "But let's get one of those cans of tomato soup open."

The food from the hut kept us going through a lean time of hunting — we'd been in the area for too long to hope for any easy meat. I shot three more goats out of Brave Goat Creek, and a few more pigs by hunting further away all the time, but it was getting harder. We were nearly down to eating possum several times.

I got lost one day and nearly spent the night in the bush. I had no idea where I was, but just on dark I dropped down off a ridge and came out on the creek bed just where I'd lit a fire a few days earlier to have a brew. I reached camp an hour after dark, but I didn't say anything to Uncle Hec about getting bushed. I was supposed to be able to remember exactly where I was at all times.

Uncle Hec's foot was improving, especially after we changed the shirtsleeves for a proper bandage. He could take a bit of weight on it and get around more easily, but he still couldn't get his boot on. It made him real crotchety, that foot. I was reading *Don Quixote* again and he used to say it was turning my head. But he was only looking for something to grumble about. It's a good book, that.

The winter was half-over by the time he could walk on his foot again. We were down to fried eel and damper by this time and the dogs were definitely eating better than we were. We'd been at Broken-foot Camp for just under eight weeks and we would have to move on soon to stay eating. As a matter of fact I suspected I was losing weight from not enough to eat. My pants were getting loose.

We made it to the Te Pua hut the first day and had to do a starve for another few days because we'd overdone it on Uncle Hec's foot. When we got to the Tauwharana hut we finally found some food — flour, rice, powdered milk, instant mashed potato, and half a tin of golden syrup. There was a notice on the wall. I read it out.

To Hector William Faulkner, of Apopo Valley Road, Gisborne County: You are required to present yourself and Richard Morehu Baker at the nearest police station immediately. If you have failed to comply with this order within fourteen days of June 30th, you will be deemed to be a fugitive from the law and a warrant will be issued for your immediate arrest.

N. Craddock,
Clerk of the Court,
Gisborne County.

Note: Any person or persons offering assistance to the above-named in any way renders himself/ themselves liable to a fine not exceeding 1,000 dollars or a maximum of six months imprisonment.

Here it was again. Other people interfering with us. Uncle Hec tore the poster off the wall and used it to light the fire.

"They're getting serious," he said. "We'll have to be more careful from now on."

I liked the way Uncle Hec never thought of giving in. And judging by the number of notices we found they must have stuck one of them in just about every hut in the Urewera.

There was no going back now. We were fugitives from the law. Our freedom was threatened.

CHAPTER
SIX

A
FRIEND

As we made our way through the bush we developed a new set of rules. We had to assume that every ranger, forestry worker, hunter, tramper and chopper pilot would know about us and be on the watch for us. The track-cutting gangs didn't worry us.

"The only thing that makes more noise than a track-cutter in the bush is a helicopter," said Uncle Hec.

We weren't so concerned about the possum trappers, either.

"Anyone who'd leave a camp full of skins and walk out to report us to the cops wouldn't be very bright," Uncle Hec pointed out. "Possum trappers don't dob people in as a rule, anyway. They've usually got more to worry about."

Whenever we travelled on a main track we made it a rule that one of us went fifty or sixty metres ahead. It cut down on any talking and it gave us a chance for the one behind to get out of sight if we ran into anyone. We agreed to brush our teeth and have a proper wash at least every two days, in case we slipped into getting dirty without noticing.

Uncle Hec kept his beard down to bristles with a little pair of scissors we'd found in one of the huts. Before that we'd been giving each other haircuts by setting fire to each other's hair with a candle and brushing it out before it went too far, with not very good results.

We were getting better at knowing where to find supplies of food. Some of the huts were always being replenished by trampers and hunters who spent their last night in the bush there. And there were huts that never seemed to have anything in them at all. It always worked out that the more food, the more people, and the risk of being spotted by someone and we'd have to move away to some other part of the Urewera. But we were certainly eating better now we could move around.

When it rained we usually sneaked up and checked out one of the huts, and if there was no one around we'd move in and make ourselves comfortable. It was fairly safe to stay in a hut while the rivers were flooded because no one could get through the tracks. The choppers hardly ever stopped at the huts — they cost too much to run for any flying time that wasn't hunting. They had to catch an animal an hour just to cover their costs and we'd heard that most of them were having a struggle to stay in business. The price of live deer was about half what it was the year before and lifting out venison didn't cover the cost of running the machine. We never had much to do with the chopper people; they lived in a different world from us.

On fine days we often camped on a bush terrace up a side creek somewhere and slept or read books until it was dark and safe to light a fire. At night it was a different matter. We had the whole Urewera to ourselves and could wander round in the open and build up huge fires if we felt like it. We even talked louder at night, to make up for the whispers of the daytime. We were becoming nocturnal.

Another thing we discovered was that the paradise duck, the putangitangi, had changed from being a noisy nuisance to a perfect alarm system. No one can sneak up on a paradise duck, apart perhaps from an abo, and we found that if we camped on their territory they'd fly up and down kicking up a mighty racket for about half an hour. Then they'd settle down again, but remain super alert. Whenever anyone else appeared from any direction the ducks would warn us in time for us to grab our gear and disappear into the bush before they could get within sight. We had only one genuine alarm from the putangitangi, and some false ones, but you could relax a few notches when you knew they were there watching out for you.

Towards the end of the winter the pigs, our main meat, became skinnier and more scarce until we couldn't find any anywhere. Even Uncle Hec had given up guessing where they might be. In the finish we had to go right out to the edge of the bush and compete with the weekend hunters to get a bit of decent pork. Then the rain made us go back to one of the huts.

We did have one memorable feed about that time. We were skimming through some of the best huts but there weren't many people in the bush at that time of year. The last thing we'd eaten was half a weka each and a packet of instant noodles we'd found in the Onepu hut — and that was hours before. We crossed the Kahikatea Range and dropped down a steep shingly tawa creek-head of the Otapukawa Stream. And suddenly we saw dozens of wood-pigeons eating the miro berries. We were going to eat.

We chose a good spot in a grove of miro trees and waited for the pigeons to come flapping in, whistling with weight, to land on the branches. Then we plonked them with the .22. They were so fat that some of them burst, an inch of bright yellow fat all over them, when they hit the ground. When we had eight of them we set up our camp by a trickle of water and smothered the birds in clay (feathers and guts and all) until they looked in the firelight like a row of loaves of bread. Then we rolled them into the embers of the fire and built it up around them. We waited for just over an hour before raking them out and breaking them open like Easter eggs. The feathers came away with the clay, as did most of the skin. They were falling apart and were very delicious and tasty. Uncle Hec ate two on his own while the Bird-lady and I ate one and a half each. The rest of them we wrapped in leaves and took with us when we moved on to Manuoha the next day.

Next we visited a few more huts before sheltering from the rain at Hautapu for two days. When the weather cleared we headed towards the northern end of the Urewera to meet the spring. And on the way there we had our worst argument ever.

We'd been walking for hours with heavy packs and we'd come down the wrong ridge off the Maungataniwha Range and found ourselves in a steep, waterfally, log-jammed, bush-lawyery, slippery little creek.

"I told you we should have gone further along the main range," I told Uncle Hec.

He looked back at me up some rocks he had just slid down beside a waterfall and said, "If you tell me that once more I'll flatten you, you smart little bastard."

"You're wrong and you won't admit it," I said. "You snore, too!"

"I hit pretty hard as well," he said, looking dangerous.

"You'd better not hit me," I told him.

He jumped forward grabbing at my leg and I got out of the way just in time. If he'd got hold of me then he'd have flattened me all right. I ran back up the creek a few yards for a head start, but he didn't come after me. We stood looking over this waterfall at each other for a while, and then he turned and walked off down the creek.

"Come on then," I think he said, and that was the last thing either of us said to each other for two days and nights, which was a bit hard-case considering what happened to us just after that. When we finally crawled out of the mouth of that creek and set off up the river towards

Central Waiau hut, we suddenly heard a strange noise, so we stopped.

The trees were shivering. The ground was shaking and trembling under our feet. The movement got heavier and suddenly we were in the middle of a great big earthquake. Dislodged rocks started crashing off a bluff above us, hurtling down through the bush and bounding out into the air, breaking up and landing all round us. All we could do was watch them coming and try to dodge the rocks of all sizes and shapes pelting like rain at us. On the other side something big crashed into the river but we were too busy to dare look round, even when rotten broken lumps of wood flew out past me onto the stones. Then we were up to our ankles in water. The riverbed had lifted and pushed the water out across the shingle flat, before draining away again.

Then the earthquake stopped. Just like that. There was no time even to get scared. One moment we were being belted with rocks pelting all round us and the river was going mad, the next everything was back to normal again, except the stones were wet, a big dead matai tree had fallen across the river and its shattered branches were lying scattered around, and there was broken rock everywhere. Otherwise it was hard to believe what we'd just seen happening. I looked at Uncle Hec to see what he was going to say about it, but he didn't say anything at all until two nights later when we were over in the Whakatane Valley.

It had rained half the night and most of the day and we'd dropped down to the river in another of Uncle Hec's bad places and found it flooded from bank to bank. We had to cross if we didn't want to spend the night in the rain. There was a big Forestry hut half an hour downstream on the other side and we had some rice and powdered milk stashed in a plastic bag near there.

We would normally have stopped and talked about it but this time Uncle Hec didn't even pause. He walked straight out into the current and let it carry him waist-deep across to the sweep of the bend on the far side. By this time I'd felt my way out into the current as well and suddenly the force grabbed my legs and I had to go with it, running in slow-motion under the brown water, bobbing downstream in the surge of it, easing my way across the stones towards the far side, already well downstream of Uncle Hec.

Suddenly I was in serious trouble. A broken-off branch started to sweep and roll along with me, carrying me right down the rapids under the water, rolling round and round and then out into a big swirl with my pack the only thing that floated me upright, and then down into another straight. Just when I thought I was going to fall through the next rapids my foot got a shove on a rock and I clawed and crawled and splashed my way out into shallow water where I lay coughing and gasping and realising how easy it'd be to get drowned.

Uncle Hec came hurrying over and dragged me onto my feet. I coughed up some water I'd swallowed.

"Next time you can do that on your own," I said between coughs.

"Next time we'll wait for the river to go down a bit, eh," he said.

And we were talking again.

≈

Springtime came and then disappeared for a week before returning. We'd made it through the winter. All of a sudden there were deer and pigs in every creek and riverbed; the huts were stocked with new food, and a new clutch of helicopters slapped their way across the ridges every night and morning. The Urewera was coming alive again, and the dawn chorus of the birds became noisier every day. There were people everywhere, but with plenty to eat we had the leisure to be able to keep out of their way. It was a quiet life after the hassles of the winter, and in spite of having to be extra careful we soon had stocks of food stashed near several of the huts in case of emergencies. We also knew the location of the keys to four of the Forestry food cupboards which had just been stocked up for the summer season. We had plenty of food for the time being, but I wasn't going to forget the lessons of Broken-foot Camp for a while.

We'd been sleeping by a creek on a grassy bank one day until the sandflies drove us awake, when we sidled out and waited on the bluff opposite the Koranga Forks hut until the sun went down. There was no sign of life, so we came down from the bluff in the last of the twilight. It was dark by the time we rounded the track to the hut, certain that we had the place to ourselves for the night. But Uncle Hec suddenly stopped and held up his hand to be quiet.

"What's up?" I whispered.

"Someone's been here recently," he said. "Like today. I can smell the fire. Hasn't been out long enough."

We threw a piece of wood on the roof to see if anyone was sleeping in there. No response.

"I'll go in and have a look," said Uncle Hec.

He entered the hut and I saw a match flare up and the candle flame inside.

"Come here!" he called out.

I went into the hut and saw a man lying on one of the bunks. I thought he must have been dead at first, but his arm hanging over the side of the bunk twitched in the candlelight.

"What's wrong with him?" I said, peering.

"Don't know. Hold this candle."

Uncle Hec bent over the man and gave him a shake.

"Hey, mate. Wake up."

He was a big young man, bleary and pale and unshaven. He stank a bit. His eyes opened into wet slits and he looked towards us, trying to say something, but no sound came out.

"This bloke's crook," said Uncle Hec. "Get some wood and water in here and I'll get a fire going."

We found another candle and when I came back from the creek with a billy of water Uncle Hec poured some into a mug and tried to get the sick man to drink. But he started coughing and choking and I thought he was going to die right then. Then he lay back gasping and seemed to go to sleep again.

"Let's have a brew, anyway," said Uncle Hec.

"What's wrong with him?" I whispered.

"No idea, but he's not going to last much longer, by the look of him."

"What'll we do?"

"One of us'll have to go out and get a chopper in for him. There's a sheep station about an hour and a half up the Koranga from here. Good track all the way. Someone'll have to go out and get them to ring up for a chopper at daylight. Don't know if this rooster's going to last till then, but it's the best we can do."

"We'll both go," I suggested.

"No," he said. "One of us ought to stay here and make sure he doesn't choke or something."

"I'll go then," I said, not really liking the idea of being left alone in the hut with the dying man and half a candle.

"Okay," said Uncle Hec. "We'll get a feed into you and I'll show you where the track starts. You have to be sure to remember where it comes out of the bush at the other end. Could be tricky to find in the dark."

"I'll remember," I promised.

He cut a cross with my knife in the side of a milk-powder tin and poked a candle into it. It made a nifty torch which lit up the track in front of me brightly. I grabbed another third of a candle and some matches and I was ready.

"Yell out from above the house and wake them up. Get them to ring the police in Matawai and tell them there's a bloke dying in the Forks hut. Needs urgent medical attention . . ."

"All right," I said. "I've got it."

I powered up the track and came out on farmland almost before I was ready for it. I located the farmhouse by a light in one of the windows. Dogs started barking as I approached and I shouted "Hey! Anyone home?"

Another light came on before the door opened and a man came out into the light. I could see him but he couldn't see me and the Bird-lady in some fern up the hill.

"What's going on?" he called out, shielding his eyes and looking round.

"There's a man dying in the Forks hut," I called back. "Can you ring the police and get them to send a helicopter for him in the morning?"

"I suppose so. How long has he been sick? What's the matter with him?"

"We don't know. Just arrived there and found him. We don't know if he'll live till morning."

"Okay. I'll give 'em a ring. Would you like a cup of tea and something to eat?"

It was a thrilling idea but . . . "No thanks. I'll have to get back. You'll ring up then?"

"Sure. You can come in and ring them yourself if you like. We won't eat you."

"No, thanks," I called back, and dropped over onto the road to go back to the track, because I could tell that no one was going to chase after me. All the same that Bird-lady had me ready to leap up the bank into the bush at the first sound of a motor starting up behind me.

It wasn't so good going back to the hut. I was worn out and down to my last stub of spare candle when I stumbled across the swingbridge and into the hut. Uncle Hec revived me with tea and scone-loaf and a tin of lambs' tongues.

The man was still alive. He'd been awake for a few minutes and had drunk some tea. Uncle Hec had been able to make out that he was a diabetic, but he hadn't been able to say any more than that.

I'd never read anything about diabetics, and Uncle Hec didn't know about them either.

"I think it's got something to do with sugar," he said. "Anyway it looks like he might just hang on till morning. You're sure they're going to ring up?"

I nodded. "Far as I could tell."

"We'd better be ready for them then. They might just try to grab us along with our patient here."

We stashed our packs in the bush behind the hut before I slept. When Uncle Hec woke me with a feed before daylight, the sick man hadn't stirred, but he was still breathing. I stood outside with my mug of tea, listening. Then I caught a faint vibration in the air down the valley.

"Chopper!" I yelled.

"Right," said Uncle Hec. "Let's go."

He took a quick look at the man on the bunk and we grabbed our packs and climbed up onto the ridge in the bush, keeping the dogs close in behind. We'd just settled down when a Hughes 500 dived in and landed by the hut. Two men in overalls jumped out and ran ducking under the blades to the hut. Then they came back to fetch a stretcher from the chopper and brought the sick man out on it and loaded him into the machine. Soon they lifted off and climbed away down the valley.

"Hope he makes it," said Uncle Hec.

"What now?" I asked.

"Well, they know we're around here somewhere. If they're going to try and round us up this'd be a good time for them to try."

He thought for a while. "I reckon if we climbed back onto that bluff where we were yesterday we could keep an eye on the place and see what happens."

"Won't that be dangerous?"

"No more than anything else we do. They'd be expecting us to be an hour away from here by this time, but I wouldn't put it past them to try and catch us. Let's move."

We cut round to the Kahanui branch and left a few footprints leading upstream, before coming back down, walking in the water, and climbing up onto the bluff opposite the hut. No sooner had we tied the dogs up in some fern when the same chopper dropped back in and let four men off, three of them with rifles. Then the chopper took off again, up the Kahanui, and two of the men went up the Koranga and the others up the ridge behind the hut.

By the time they were out of sight Uncle Hec was curled up in his sleeping-bag among some tree-roots. He hadn't slept all the previous night. I had some cheese and bread before climbing into my sleeping-bag and falling asleep too.

The sound of the chopper returning woke us up. It was late afternoon and the last of the sun was just leaving our level. Down in the shadow we saw the four men get into the chopper before it lifted off. It flew right past where we were crouched in the fern and as soon as it had gone we gathered our gear together, untied the dogs and went back to the hut for a feed of rice risotto, beef noodles, buttered damper and condensed milk in our tea.

We both felt indignant about them searching for us like that, so we hung around the Forks hut till we'd eaten nearly all the food there. Then we took it easy up the Kahanui River to Tawa hut where there was someone installed so we watched from a low ridge downstream. A short dark man came out of the hut and started chopping wood. Uncle Hec knew him, he was an old trapping mate of his called Brian — Quiet Brian, because he never talked much. There was no one else about so we went down and said g'day and had a big feed of his meat and spuds.

Quiet Brian had been trapping around Tawa all winter and he had a good line of skins. He'd done well and was going to pay off his house in Gisborne this trip. He had plenty of supplies and no one else had been there for weeks, so we camped with him for a few days and gave him a hand tacking out skins and shifting a line of traps. He'd been warned by the rangers to keep a lookout for us.

The first night we were there Quiet Brian cooked up some juicy venison steaks in his cast-iron camp-oven — very nice. I ate a whole back-steak on my own, about fifteen pieces. Next day he was showing us his possum-skin set-up in a separate shed when Uncle Hec noticed the big bulge in the muslin cloth hanging dripping into a dirty yoghurt pottle.

"What's this?" he said.

"Possum fat," said Quiet Brian. "I put all the scrapings off my skins through it. Strains it."

"What for?" I asked uneasily.

"I do all my cooking in it," he said.

I suddenly recognised the unfamiliar taste I'd noticed about the venison the night before. Quiet Brian's maggoty possum skins! I was just about sick, and I never ate anything out of his oven after that. Instead I found an old aluminium frying pan and cleaned it up to cook my stuff in. Quiet Brian was genuinely sorry for me, not being able to digest possum fat like that. Uncle Hec didn't like it, either. He went out in the rain one day and came back with a whole mutton. Plenty of proper dripping to cook in, but you could still tell that Quiet Brian actually preferred possum fat.

It would have been nice to stay on at Tawa for a while; it was so peaceful I started feeling ordinary again. But after eight days Uncle Hec became uneasy about the possibility of other people being around and we decided to move on. Quiet Brian and Uncle Hec swapped boots and arranged for Quiet Brian to leave a packhorse of supplies under a certain bank for us. He wouldn't let us pay him anything for them and seemed really sad when we parted. The dogs were sad too — they were so full of possum they could hardly walk.

I liked Quiet Brian, he was our friend — maybe our only friend in all that bush. I didn't realise why Uncle Hec was so keen to get away from him until we ran into a bunch of people less than an hour away from Tawa, heading in that direction. If they'd found us camped there Quiet Brian would have been liable to a maximum fine of 1,000 dollars or a term of imprisonment not exceeding six months.

There were four people in the party and they sprang us out on the open riverbed. They were trampers — two girls, a boy and an older man. Uncle Hec employed his usual evasive tactics and kept walking straight towards them without altering stride. I followed him and as we walked past them one of the girls said, "Ooooh — it's them! The ones the police are looking for!"

"Shhhhh!" said the older man.

And we just kept walking until we were clear of them.

We'd now been seen twice in the same valley in two weeks, so we struck out for the far side of the Urewera, and six days later we rested up in a wreck of a hut in the Mokomokonui. At night we could hear the trucks grinding over the Taupo–Napier Highway, but we were as safe here as anywhere else we could think of, except, perhaps, at Broken-foot Camp.

There some fat wild sheep in the Mokomokonui so we stayed there for ten days and took a big supply of roasted mutton with us when we moved on. It was good to know we didn't have to catch a pig or go hungry. We had so much meat we didn't know what to do with it.

Uncle Hec had talked about a hot pool beside a creek on an old deer block of his, and on a scrounging trip through the Hautapu I talked him into making a detour. It was a two-day walk and he wasn't sure if it was still there or not, but we eventually found it. You could smell the sulphur everywhere, but it took us a while to find the actual hot water, a red seepage steaming at the bottom of a bank a few feet from the creek.

It took us a good hour to clear enough stones out of the hole for us to bathe, and we found that it filled up with seepage from the creek almost as fast as we could dig it. We were wet and white-fingered by the time we'd hollowed the bath out and all we had for our trouble was a patch of smelly tepid water at one edge of a big hole full of pure cold bush creek. We'd had it for the day.

We found a site just downstream where there was plenty of firewood and risked a big warm-up. Next morning light rain and sleet was falling and it was very wet and gloomy. I wandered up to have a look at the big hole we'd dug the day before and the whole surface was steaming. It had hotted up during the night. I swirled my hand through it and started yelling out for Uncle Hec.

We could just stand the heat in the cooler water near the creek, but the electric flakes of sleet drove us deeper like nails into the hot water, right up to our ears. It took half an hour to ease our way over to the hot edge near the bank, before we staggered out steaming like ghosts in the rain until the cold started stinging through and we slipped back into the hot water again.

When we'd had too much of the experience we fumbled weakly around, pulling our clothes on and building up a big fire to dry everything out. I had one more soak in the hot pool later that day when the rain stopped, but Uncle Hec said he was already soggy enough and gave it a miss. Three days later at Pohukura we still stank of sulphur, but it was worth it to have had that mighty bath.

From Pohukura we moved across into the Waiau Valley, and it was there, in the Te Waiotukapiti hut, that they finally caught us.

CHAPTER
SEVEN

SERIOUS
TROUBLE

It had been raining on and off all that day, so we stayed in the Te Waiotukapiti hut, burning a big pile of tawa branches we'd thrown down out of the bush. Uncle Hec was cutting up the last of the mutton to add to a stew and I was re-reading *The Thorn Birds*. The main sound was the rain spattering onto the roof through trees. It was cosy and peaceful.

One of the dogs barked once and suddenly three big young men were standing in the hut, dripping water. Two of them had rifles with telescopic sights, and it wasn't cosy and peaceful any more. My main thought was how different from us they looked. I could smell some kind of scented soap off them. They dropped their packs on the floor and introduced themselves: Hugh, Joe and Ron, all National Park rangers, checking the tracks and huts in the area.

"Stinks in here," the one called Ron said, looking up and down us.

We didn't say anything. They got out mugs and filled them from our billy over our fire and had tea, sitting on the edges of the bunks. The one called Hugh seemed to be their leader.

"You two are supposed to be over in the Waioeka," he said.

"First I heard of it," said Uncle Hec.

"You were seen over there about a month ago."

"No kidding."

"Come on, old man. We know who you are. You're Faulkner, and this is Baker. We knew we'd pick you up sooner or later."

"That a fact?"

"You're caught, you might as well admit it."

"What are you going to do about it?"

"We'll have to take you out to the base, of course."

"Why?"

"Because you're wanted, that's why."

"Who wants us?"

"The police, that's who."

"You're not the police."

"No, we're Park Board rangers."

"Then *you* don't want us."

"Not us personally. We've got nothing against you. We know the guy you looked after at the Koranga Forks. We're all grateful to you for that."

"Leave us alone then."

I could tell they had no intention of leaving us alone. These heroes were going to bring us in and give us to the Social Welfare department and the police, no matter what we said or did.

"You're just making it tougher on yourselves," the one called Hugh went on. "The longer you keep up this attitude you'll only make it worse."

"You're the worst thing that's happened to us for months," Uncle Hec told him.

"Well, you've had your bit of fun. You can come out with us in the morning and get it over with."

"We'll be coming out when we're ready."

"We don't want to tie you up, old man, but we will if we have to. If you try sneaking away we'll tie you and young baggy-britches here to a tree until we're ready to march you out to the road. The party's over, old man." And he grinned around at his mates.

The one called Joe took our .22 off a bunk, checked it, and put it with theirs behind the door.

"What do you shoot with this thing — sparrows?" They laughed.

I didn't like these men. They were casual about us, as though we were already locked up. It looked as though it was the end of the party all right. Even Uncle Hec could see how hopeless it was. He sat on the edge of a bunk and said nothing, while the rangers muttered among themselves, not really caring if we heard or not. The one called Ron wanted to tie us up, but the other two said to wait unless we made it necessary.

"They're harmless," one of them said. And still Uncle Hec didn't say anything.

Whenever either of us moved, one of them would shift between us and the door. If we had go outside two of them came with us — we were prisoners. They took it in turns to sit by the door in front of the rifles, in case we tried making a run for it. When I climbed into my sleeping-bag that night, topping and tailing with Uncle Hec on the same bunk, I couldn't sleep for hours. I was worried as I'd ever been, and wished that something really nasty would happen to those rangers, like a meteorite crashing through the roof of the hut and breaking all their legs.

I must have gone to sleep in the end, because the next thing I heard was Uncle Hec calling out my name. I sat up and so did the three rangers. The one in the chair by the door was the last to wake up. It was just getting light.

Uncle Hec called out again from outside. "Ricky!"

"What?" I yelled back, getting out of my sleeping-bag.

"Get out here!"

I knew something critical was on, as did the rangers. I went to the door and they crowded behind me, a big hand grabbing me above the elbow and holding me there. It had stopped raining and the whole valley was sodden and soaked in mist. Uncle Hec was standing by the woodblock with the .22 in one hand.

"Grab our packs and load 'em up, Ricky. We're snatching it from here, and if one of those blokes touches you, yell out and get under the end bunk quick."

"He's mad," muttered one of the rangers, and I had to agree it looked like it. Uncle Hec can look very hot round the eyes when he gets in that mood of his.

"You boys just keep out of our way. Anyone touches one of us, gets it."

The grip round my arm slid away.

"You've done it now," the one called Hugh said. "You realise . . ."

"I know what I'm doing, sonny. You just keep right out of the way and you won't get hurt. Ricky, move it!"

I ducked round them into the hut and started stuffing our gear into the packs. No one tried to stop me; they were still standing at the door, talking to Uncle Hec, so I scooped a few cans of their food into our packs.

"You wouldn't shoot us," the one called Joe said.

"You just try me, young feller," said Uncle Hec. "You're easier to hit than a sparrow. I'd drop you before you could move."

I didn't like going too near him, but I lugged our packs in his direction.

"Get the dogs."

I untied them and we picked up our packs and moved away downstream, looking back to make sure they didn't come after us.

"What have you done with our rifles?" one of them shouted.

"Under the hut," called back Uncle Hec. "And if any of you try following us you'll deserve what you get."

"You'll never get away with this," the one called Hugh yelled after us, and then we were out of sight of them and free again.

Two crossings down the river we climbed up onto a bush spur, dropped our packs, tied up the dogs and sat against a tree for a while. I was still shaky. When we'd had a spell we sidled back past the hut up in the bush and found a place in some ferns where we could watch the main track out to the road.

"What happens now?" I said.

"It could get a bit tricky for a while. My bet is that they'll head straight out and raise the alarm."

"Would you have shot them?" I couldn't help asking.

"Hard to say. Shut up, they're due past here any time now."

About half an hour later the three rangers came up the track and passed by thirty feet below. They weren't trying to follow us, but you could tell by their faces and the way they were half-running that Uncle Hec and I were in trouble with other people again. Serious trouble this time.

When they had gone we went back to the hut and took all the food and books it could spare and carried them in a sack to where we'd left our packs and dogs. Then we climbed up through the dripping bush onto the Pukekohu Range and camped that night on a flat rock by the Manganuiohou River on the other side.

Next morning, right on daylight, it started. Choppers swept up and down the valley, slapping across the tree-tops, and others came and went dropping people off at various vantage points. It was as well for us that there weren't many places where they could land, but we had to be particularly careful of the choppers because we knew some of them had infra-red gear that could pick up an animal or a person, so we had to stay in deep bush, the tall timber.

We never used to put more than three or four bullets in the magazine of the rifle at once, but this day Uncle Hec put the full fifteen in and stuck a handful of extra ones in his pocket, so I knew we were in for a heavy day. I was scared.

We worked our way round to a ridge that would take us further away from most of the activity and after a couple of hours we were just coming up onto the crest of the ridge when we became suspicious. The birds were too quiet. We stopped to listen and we'd just looked at each other to see whether we should move on when we heard a radio crackle and hiss up on the ridge and someone call out, "I'm over here!" We knew there was more than one of them, so we sidled away through the bush and tried the only direction we had left.

It can make you nervous, hiding day and night. We had to stay super-quiet, and couldn't talk above a whisper for days and nights. Every now and again we walked for a few minutes up a side creek and then doubled back in the water, in case they were tracking us with dogs. Willy and Zag must have thought we were crazy that day, as they weren't even allowed to chase nice fat pigs that jumped up right in front of us.

We heard some shots and shouting out on our left on another ridge and eased away from there. The main search seemed to be concentrated over in the Waiau and Te Hoe valleys, and it looked as though they'd guessed we'd gone that way, but then they swung round in a wide circle and surrounded us. We were cut off from the main part of the Urewera.

This was serious. We stashed some of our load where we could find it again and set off on a mad game of hide and seek through 25,000 hectares of bush and streams and ridges and slips and waterfalls and cliffs.

For three days we dodged them back and forth across the

watershed, using Uncle Hec's strategy of sticking around to keep an eye on what everyone else was up to. There was always the chance that we might try it once too often, and that we might be caught any moment, any hour. They had dogs this time too — we'd heard them bark a few times. The dogs must have known we were still around there somewhere, but they kept losing our trail, because we kept them a mile behind us, running up and down false trails.

"Them kinda dogs can't wind-find in the bush," whispered Uncle Hec. "They have to track you."

So we formed a pattern and used it every now and then, especially if we'd heard any barking close by. We'd look at each other, nod, and then split up and go in opposite directions, round into a side-creek and back to the main stream, walking in the water. The scent of our dogs only seemed to add to the confusion behind us. When we needed a rest we'd climb up into a steep creek-head somewhere and rest up, listening to make sure they didn't come too close.

There were certainly plenty of people and choppers and dogs. It took them only a few minutes to pick people up and drop them right over on the other side of the watershed, so they could get from behind us to in front of us before we could move 200 metres. They only needed to sight us once and surround us, but they were so clumsy and noisy in the bush that we could always tell where they were. Some of them actually shouted out to one another.

"They couldn't track an elephant through six feet of snow, those clowns," whispered Uncle Hec, looking down at the bushes thrashing around down in the gully, where someone seemed to be getting tangled up in the supplejack. But the people waiting on the ridges with radios were a bigger worry. Twice we smelt cigarette smoke and had to Bird-lady it in a wide circle around them.

They still should have caught us. One evening we were looking for somewhere to camp on a bush flat along the bottom of a ridge, and we heard these two bushmen thumping and cracking and snapping in their big boots down the ridge. We stood in a clump of pepperwoods and watched them come tripping and fumbling down the ridge and onto the flat. They stopped about forty metres away in the trees and started talking loud about which way to go. One of them had a rifle and the other a radio on his belt. They were arguing. They were lost. Suddenly a vine I must have been half-standing on flicked up and hit Willy on the nose. He yelped.

"What was that?" said one of the bushmen.

"I didn't say anything," said the other one.

And they took off through the bush, no doubt to spend the night in the open because the hut they were looking for was nearly two hours in the other direction. But that's how alert they were.

We ate everything we had with us. It was cold, with no fires and no tea. We slept curled up in our bags in the roots of totara or rata trees — they're the warmest. It can make you very tired and hungry, living like that, and we were very relieved when the search spread out and away from us, deeper into the Urewera. Uncle Hec was right. They didn't think we'd be game to stick so close to where we'd been caught. They thought we must have got through to the main part of the Urewera.

On the fourth day we came up out of the tall timber and pushed and pulled each other and the dogs up onto the Kotare Ridge up a tricky gully. We didn't want to try the leading ridges because they were still too dangerous. We picked our way towards the southern end of the bush, away from most of the activity. It was real Bird-lady sneaking. Uncle Hec went in front and I kept him just in sight through the bush. The cover got a bit scattery in places and we had to dive for it whenever we heard a chopper come too close. They had a habit of coming suddenly up over a ridge or round a corner and they could be on you before you knew what was happening if you didn't watch out. I'd never been so nervous of a patch of open ground in my life.

We travelled along the Kotare for two and a half hours, heading for a place Uncle Hec knew about from when he'd hunted goats there in 1966, but he was having trouble remembering exactly how to get there. After casting around for a while we found a place — all second-growth manuka and grassy clearings, with shelfed bluffs and rocky slips — where we could get over the side. We kept to the high ground and came out on a wide shelf where the bluff fell away to open sheep country. We could see anything coming for miles up there, and there were three directions of escape.

We made our camp under a big dry overhang of rock, almost a cave, and by dark that night we were invisible behind a wall of rocks and scrub.

"The only thing we can do now is wait," said Uncle Hec. "When they've burnt 'emselves out looking for us in there we'll get back over to the Ruakituri or somewhere."

We saw two lots of four-wheel-drive vehicles go up the valley next morning and come back out again in the evening. There was a lot of chopper activity, but none came near. It looked as though we had them tricked — it was a good place all right. We called it Cave Camp. We ate a lot of hares there, when it was safe to shoot, and there were two different mobs of goats further round the bluff. There was a gully full of pig-rooting half an hour up the Otoi side, and plenty of sheep down on the grass if we got desperate.

We didn't like to steal sheep off the farmers around the edges of the bush because it would have turned them against us, and we had enough enemies as it was, but the mutton was always there as a backstop. There was no need to swipe mutton at Cave Camp, as it turned out. The worst thing was being stuck up there not being able to move around. We lay around all day, reading and sleeping, and as soon as the last chopper had gone past down the valley we could let the dogs off and come out into the open, where we could sit round the fire eating and talking till the early hours of the morning.

We could tell when they scaled down the hunt for us as though they'd told us. The choppers stopped blatting around all over the place and the only ones left went straight up the valley and came out again with deer slung underneath. They weren't looking for people. The vehicles and people stopped going up and down the valley, and anyway we knew without any of that. It felt different to walk round in the open daylight.

We were now low on food, so Uncle Hec made a trip back to the hut where we'd got caught, Te Waiotukapiti, and got back next day with a packful of flour and tinned food, plus packets and sachets, a dozen eggs, a bottle of tomato sauce and extra salt. He even brought some books. He'd also shot a deer just along the Kotare Ridge and hung it in a tree, so we had plenty to eat.

Clearly they'd been using the Te Waiotukapiti hut as a base while they were looking for us, and they'd stocked it up well. Uncle Hec had stashed another load of food near the hut for next time. There was still untouched hunting around us, and we had plenty of time to sort out the camp. We put in a punga screen, disguised it with ferns, and built our fire so that the smoke went up the face of the bluff and you couldn't tell it from the mist, if there was any of that about, which was just about every morning. We built our bunks up with mingi-mingi vines till they were like my inner-sprung back at the farm. We collected our water from a spring in a clump of fern thirty metres round the base of the bluff, and there was more dead manuka around than even Uncle Hec could burn.

The only bad thing about Cave Camp was that it was so high up you always had to climb up to it with whatever you'd caught or shot.

It was a long drag at the end of a hunt, but it was worth it once you were up there.

When it was time to go back to Te Waiotukapiti for more supplies we both went, taking the dogs and the books to exchange. We tied the dogs on the ridge above the hut and went down to find no one around. They'd stocked up the hut *again*.

There were candles, which we were short of, and tins of peas and cheese and meat and puddings, plus an unopened ten-kg bag of self-raising flour — but only one book this time. Uncle Hec showed me where he'd stashed the other stuff, in a hole under a big rata's roots, so we added more to it and left it there for next time. Then we each carried a good load home — and there was still plenty left. A good hut, that.

We returned to Cave Camp in the dark and had a big meal of stewed apricots with condensed milk and tins of chocolate pudding. Everything tastes good when you've been walking for nine hours across the Kotare. It's what Uncle Hec called a "gutbuster".

We soon got to know all the country where everything was for hours in every direction from Cave Camp, except the farmhouse you could see down in the valley from the end of the bluff. Someone was living down there but he or she never came up our way and we'd given up worrying about them. Then we went and got caught again.

This is how it happened. We'd been down at the river doing some washing and we were climbing up one of our main tracks back to Cave Camp when we came across a set of horse's hoofprints going straight up towards the camp. *Shod* hoofprints. I was getting ready to run for it, but Uncle Hec said to hold it, so I held it, and we sneaked up and had a look.

A horse with a saddle on was feeding outside the cave and a man with a woolly hat was leaning there. We watched him for a while.

He was a big young man, a clean one, the sort that always meant trouble for us. Then Uncle Hec stood up.

"Come on," he said. "We'll go and see what he wants. We've got a gun and he hasn't."

I was shaky with apprehension as we walked over to meet the stranger. Every time something like this happened our lives tended to take a violent swerve in another direction. There was sadness, too. We'd got to like our Cave Camp; it was safe and comfortable and easy living, but because this man was standing there it could never be any of those things to us any more.

"G'day," said Uncle Hec.

"Hello there," said the man, smiling a bit.

"What brings you up here?" asked Uncle Hec, leaning the rifle against the rock.

"Seeing as we've been neighbours for the past few weeks I thought it was about time we got acquainted. My name's Rob Barton — they call me Robby."

He shook hands with Uncle Hec and I moved out of the way and started pushing the embers of the fire together in case he tried to shake hands with me too.

"This your place here?" asked Uncle Hec.

"No, I'm caretaking the place for the stock and station agents. It's a bankrupt sheep station and I'm keeping it more or less running till they decide what they want to do with it."

"How long have you known we were here?"

"Since a few days after you got away from the Park Board boys," he said.

"Anyone else know we're here?"

He shook his head. "Only me. I'm on my own down there."

"How did you find us?"

"Don't worry, it was a sheer fluke. I was looking across the bluffs to see where the goats were, I use them for dog-tucker sometimes, and I spotted your mate here and his dogs digging a possum out of the flax up on the shelf there. They still had the big search on at the time, so I left you alone until it died down. You're safe enough now, though. You were supposed to have broken into a bach over on the Te Kaha coast a couple of days ago. I'm pretty sure no one suspects you're anywhere near here."

"*You* know we're here," pointed out Uncle Hec. "That's not no one."

"If I was going to turn you in I'd have done it before this," he said. "Look, how would you two like to come down to the homestead for a meal and a bath. I've just got some food in and you look as though you could do with a clean-up and a change of clothes."

"No thanks, mate," said Uncle Hec. "We're okay the way we are. We'd appreciate it if you'd give us a day or two to get well away from here, that's all."

"Okay, suit yourself," the man called Robby said, "but I've got some information you ought to know."

"What?"

"I'll tell you in private."

"You can say anything you like in front of my mate," said Uncle Hec.

"— there's a price on your head."

Even the horse stopped eating and looked up.

"How much?" said Uncle Hec.

"Two thousand five hundred dollars for information leading to your apprehension. There's already been a few parties gone in looking for you, hoping to pick up the reward. They carry two-way radios to call up the choppers if they spot you. You've been classified as dangerous, not be approached."

"What are they accusing me of?"

"Abducting a minor and presenting a firearm to facilitate escaping from lawful custody — they're the main ones. They're treating the firearm one pretty seriously. You lost quite a bit of public support over that."

"What do you mean, public support?"

"Well when you chaps first took to the bush a lot of people took your side. Didn't you know about that?"

"No. What else?"

"Well when you saved that ranger's life over at the Koranga Forks you became kind of heroes. The papers made a big thing of it."

"Was he a bloody *ranger*?"

Uncle Hec and I looked at each other, not really hearing what the man called Robby went on saying.

". . . in a diabetic coma. They only just saved him. A lot of people took your side after that, some pretty high-up types, too. They were all saying you should be left alone and they were wasting public money looking for you."

"I don't believe any of this, but go on."

"When you pulled the rifle on those Park Board rangers they declared you dangerous. They called in the Armed Offenders Squad, police with tracker dogs, the army Iroquois crowd. They even recruited members of the public. Some of their best bushmen and hunters were on the job for a while. The Forestry had men with radios in half the huts in the Urewera. None of them came up with any confirmed sightings, but you were supposed to have been seen all over the place. It's died right down just lately — a lot of people have been saying you're being hunted like animals and that sort of thing. You've still got a fair bit of public sympathy."

"It's a bit hard to believe some of that," said Uncle Hec. "But thanks anyway."

"I've kept all the newspaper cuttings I've come across lately," said the man called Robby, reaching over to pick up his horse's reins off the ground before climbing into the saddle. "I'll put an extra potato in the pot in case you feel like coming down to the house tonight. You ought to have a look over those newspaper cuttings before you take off from here. But if you don't want to you needn't worry about me telling anyone about you. I don't operate that way."

"Thanks . . . er . . . what did you say your name was, mate?"

"Robby," I reminded him, speaking for the first time in front of the stranger.

"Well thanks, Robby," said Uncle Hec. "We'll think it over and come down after dark if we decide to."

"Okay, I'll expect you if you turn up. In any case, good luck."

He rode off over the edge and about twenty minutes later we saw him ride like an ant out across the riverbed and disappear towards the red roof of the homestead.

We had either to trust that little dot down there or move away somewhere else. "He seems to know a fair bit about us," said Uncle Hec. "Some of it might just be useful, if they're that anxious to get their hands on us."

"What if it's a trap?" I asked. "All that stuff about a reward on our heads and that. I don't believe it."

"It could easily be true," said Uncle Hec. "I know blokes like that — what's his name again?"

"Robby," I told him.

". . . like that Robby, and I don't reckon he'd put us crook. I'm inclined to think he's straight up."

"What if he's not?"

"That's the risky bit. What do you reckon?"

We talked it over for a while and decided to risk it. I don't know about Uncle Hec, but it was an apprehensive decision as far as I was concerned. If other people didn't leave us alone I was going to flatten one of them one of these days. Our Cave Camp was blown now.

CHAPTER
EIGHT

ANOTHER NOTCH

But a lot happened to us that night. We sneaked up on Robby's farmhouse in the evening, and as soon as we were out in the open grass country it felt as if the whole world had changed. It was so bare everywhere — hardly a tree in sight and nowhere to hide. I would have been quite happy if Uncle Hec had changed his mind and we'd turned back to Cave Camp.

"Naked, eh!" he whispered when we were getting over the fence behind the woolshed. That's just what it feels like when you go out into the open after hiding in the bush for a year and seven weeks — naked.

We tied our dogs in the woolshed yards and whistled out from near the house, and Robby came out and took us inside, into the brightest light at night I could remember. It took a while to get used to it. We sat around the kitchen table and enjoyed the warmth while Robby made us cups of tea. We could tell that no one else was around and started to relax. Robby took a small pile of stuff torn out of newspapers from a drawer in the kitchen and we started to read.

It was hard to believe those newspaper reports were about us — probably because we didn't know exactly what had been happening. It had been a big search all right, just as Robby had said. You could tell they'd expected to round us up in the first day or two, and you could also tell they hadn't been very happy about not succeeding. One search co-ordinator had said it was highly unlikely that Faulkner and Baker could survive in the bush without outside help. Then there were some letters and editorials saying how ridiculous it was for them to be spending all that money and effort in fruitless attempts to outwit a doddering old bush rat and a half-witted youth.

Another interesting thing was that some of the journalists had declared that the Park Board rangers had had no right to detain Baker in the Te Waiotukapiti hut because there were no charges against him. One even suggested that Faulkner was within his rights to protect his nephew from being unlawfully detained. And no one could say whether the rifle had been loaded or not.

The whole collection of articles added up to a load of garbage, but it certainly gave us our first inkling of what had actually been going on and what people were saying.

We sat at the kitchen table and ate boiled beef and cabbage and bread and as much butter as we wanted. Uncle Hec and Robby talked across the other end of the table. It was the first time I'd been inside a proper house since Aunty Bella died and I didn't have much to say at first. After I'd done the dishes Robby said to help myself to a bath.

"You can use as much hot water as you like, there's tons of it. There's some clean clothes on the bed in that room there, if you feel like putting them on. They'll be a bit big for you, but they'll keep you warm."

So I went and filled the bath, and just when I was getting into it

I saw my face in the mirror. I stopped and looked at myself because we hadn't seen a proper mirror since the farm. I was pulling a few faces at myself, like you do, and then I noticed something. I looked at my body, then climbed on to the edge of the bath to get a better look in the mirror. I looked over my shoulder and turned around. I looked back at my front to make certain. There are some things you actually know about but you don't like testing them in case it turns out not to be true. This was one of those things, and it was true!

I wrapped a towel round my waist and ran out into the kitchen. Uncle Hec and Robby looked round from where they were talking with a bottle of whisky between them.

"I'm thin!" I shouted at Uncle Hec.

They just sat there.

"I'm thin," I said again.

"Yeah, I know," said Uncle Hec.

"I'm thin," I said. "You're not allowed to call me fat any more."

"I don't," he said, drinking whisky out of a tea cup. "Haven't called you that for months."

"Ever again," I said.

Robby was grinning but I didn't care.

"Depends if you get fat again," said Uncle Hec. "You're not fat so you don't get called fat."

"Why didn't you tell me?" I said. "I'm not fat any more. I'm thin!"

They were both laughing at me, but that didn't matter. Being thin can alter your whole outlook when you're used to being a fat person. I went back into the bathroom and put my thin self into the bath and had a big thin soak. I even washed my hair — a thin person's hair. I was thin all right. Thin face, thin stomach and legs and bum. Thin arms and hands. I was bony, and one of the main things I felt at the time was resentment about how long I must have been thin without realising it.

I climbed into Robby's jeans and big red woolly shirt. It was all a bit loose for a thin person like me, but the socks nearly fitted. When I came out into the kitchen Uncle Hec and Robby were deep into talk about what it was like round there in the "early days". I sat there listening to Uncle Hec talking more than I'd ever heard him, and exploring my ribs with my fingers through Robby's red woolly shirt.

I must have been yawning because Robby showed me where to sleep, in the room where the clothes were. There were two beds there, very clean-looking, with sheets and all that. I didn't like to get in the sheets so I left my clothes on and got under the top two blankets. Out in the kitchen Uncle Hec and our new friend laughed sillier and sillier with the whisky, and then I slept. Thin.

We were used to staying awake at night, but Uncle Hec wasn't used to whisky, and when he finally staggered his way to bed, shouting out to ask if I was asleep or not, he had to get up again immediately and be sick out of the window. I didn't mind, I was thin. Like Uncle Hec.

≈

We stayed at the sheep station with Robby for nearly two weeks. The first day we helped him put 2000 ewes through the spray-dip. He'd been wanting to get that done and it was too much for one man on his own. Robby had four dogs, black-and-tan ones, and they weren't bad, Uncle Hec said, but Willy and Zag were easily as good as any he had.

"You blokes have got great control over those dogs of yours," said Robby, when we were having a brew of tea and a spell at the sheepyards. "Never seen anything like it."

"You have to have 'em like that when you live the way we do," said Uncle Hec.

"How about seeing what you can do with that bitch pup of mine, Hec. She's a well-bred thing and she ought to be working by now, but I can't do a thing with her."

"I'll have a look at her," said Uncle Hec. And a few days later he had the little black-and-tan bitch, Dream, of all names, working to the whistle like a champion.

"That uncle of yours is the best man with dogs I've ever seen," said Robby one day when we were watching Uncle Hec away up the hill on a horse, bringing in 250 wethers with the help of Dream on her own.

"He's a good shot as well," I told him, feeling proud of him.

Uncle Hec and Robby shod all the station horses, eight of them, and I fixed up the fowl run and rounded up all the chooks. Robby thought we were great workers, but we were really having a good time doing ordinary things. It was like a holiday.

It rained one day and we sat round in the kitchen talking. Robby had spent a few years at Lincoln College and had managed several big sheep and cattle runs around the back country. He had a wife and two kids, girls, living with her parents in town so the kids could go to school. He used to go in and see them in his old Land Rover most weekends, and when he left us alone we were worried until he came back, alone, the following night.

He brought a load of stuff for us — boots, socks, pants, shirts and a new knife for me, as my old one was worn down to a spike. Two hundred rounds of .22 ammo, and quite a bit of other stuff. But the best of all was a transistor radio Robby said had been lying around his in-laws' place with nobody using it, and a whole box of batteries. Uncle Hec and I were a bit embarrassed by Robby's generosity. We'd agreed to let him buy us a pair of boots each till we could pay him, but the clothes and the radio and stuff were his idea. We knew he didn't have much money, and he was doing his best to help us.

Uncle Hec and I had already discussed the need for some money, to make life easier for us until I turned fifteen in nine months' time. And we owed Robby over 300 dollars already.

"I keep thinking about those possums over in the Ruakituri," said Uncle Hec. He didn't like calling it Broken-foot because it reminded him. "If they're like they were last winter you wouldn't have to get many to whack up a decent cheque."

So we made plans to trap possums at Broken-foot, up the other end of the Urewera, and pack the skins back to Robby for him to sell for us.

"I trap a few round here," he said. "Nobody'd notice if I take in a line of skins."

He was so genuine about trying to get us to stay longer at the station we had to make excuses to get away. If we were caught there we'd all be in trouble and we couldn't let Robby risk it. Twice we'd had to duck away and hide in the woolshed when cars came up the road. It was time to move.

"It's only about six weeks until the skins'll be ready," said Uncle Hec. "We'll need all that time to stock up the camp and get set up."

Robby loaded so much food and gear on us that we had to stash some of it when we got up to the Cave Camp. We stayed one night there to get our bush legs back and then headed off for Whakataka on the Huiarau Range, on our way up through the middle of the Urewera.

Life was different now. The main thing as far as I was concerned was me being thin — I even walked thin these days. But there were other important changes as well. There was a price on us now. We were wanted for a serious crime and a thing like that can alter every leaf and rock, if you let it get to you. Then there was the fact that we had new boots and clothes, socks in proper pairs without holes, and our own singlets. It gives a man respect, having a bit of decent gear.

But the thing that made the biggest difference was the radio. Whenever we camped one of the first things we did was unwrap the tranny (Uncle Hec called it the wireless) and unwind the extra aerial Robby had given us, which we'd hang in a tree and tune in to whatever we could get. Instant contact with the outside world — it was great to listen to music again. Uncle Hec hated missing the evening news and he used to get impatient when we were a bit late reaching a camping place. We half-ran down a long spur to a creek one night and just got tuned in in time to hear ourselves being mentioned on the news:

The Urewera Fugitives, Hector Faulkner, and his nephew, Richard Baker, were reportedly sighted by a tramping party in the vicinity of the Te Puna Hut, on the shores of Lake Waikaremoana yesterday. A team of police with tracker dogs was flown in to the area at first light, but no trace of the pair was found.

The officer in charge of the operation, Sergeant Bowling of the Gisborne C.I.D., told our reporter that he expected the pair to surrender themselves to the authorities by the time winter sets in properly in the mountains.

Faulkner and Baker now face their second winter in the bush. The pair have been at large now for fourteen months, and continue to frustrate all efforts to apprehend them. Anyone sighting them should not approach them, but inform the nearest police station.

That was us they were talking about.

"Fourteen months," I said to Uncle Hec. "That's a pretty long time."

"Seems longer than that to me," he said. "We've been lucky so far, but we're going to have to be more careful than ever from now on."

But in spite of us taking extra care a nasty thing happened to us one day. We were sitting in the Te Pourewa hut when we heard a chopper coming, low up the valley. We were always ready to move in a hurry, and we grabbed our stuff and were up in the bush when we heard it land at the hut. We climbed up a ridge and were about a third of the way to the top when we heard a dog bark behind us. Willy and Zag were a few yards out in front of us when we stopped and looked round. Rushing towards us was a big black Alsatian with a short lead hanging off it. It stopped to bark, then ran at us snarling. It was attacking us!

I went over one side of the ridge and Uncle Hec went over the other. I was slithering and sliding and rolling down the slope with my pack up over my head, and as I grabbed something and was getting myself the right way up, a whole tangle of dogs, Willy and Zag and the Alsatian, came rolling down the side, snarling and ripping and tearing at each other. They went sprawling down past me and ended up in a muddy wallow.

It was a fight to the death. Uncle Hec arrived and all we could do was stand and watch — there was no way we could stop them.

"Your own dog'd take a hunk out of you if you went in there," said Uncle Hec, breaking off a branch and snapping it shorter under his boot. I did the same.

The fight didn't last long. Soon Willy and Zag had the Alsatian beaten and it was yodelling and gurgling and half-drowning in the mud with no fight left in it. We dragged our dogs off, and the Alsatian got onto its feet, staggering all over the place, and limped away through the bush, dragging one front leg and yelping every now and then.

"He'll recover," said Uncle Hec. "But two of them might have been a different story."

"They're still tracking us down with dogs!" I said. "Dangerous ones!"

"Yeah. One of the choppers must have spotted us around here yesterday and put the police onto us. We'd better get the hell out of here. They mightn't be too far behind that dog, and they might have more of them. They could easily have heard that racket."

We slipped away up the ridge and hared it over into the Ruakituri where there was less chance of being disturbed, and where we worked out a plan in case we were attacked by police dogs again. Straight up a tree and if our dogs couldn't handle them we'd just have to shoot them.

"I sure hope we don't have to do that," I said.

"So do I," said Uncle Hec. "I can't think of a better way to antagonise the police than to knock off a couple of their dogs, but if they attack me I'll shoot 'em all right. Don't worry about that."

"Maybe they'll stop sending dogs after us when they see what happened to the one we sent them back."

"Start thinkin' that and you'll have one of them Alsatians swingin' off your arm before you know it."

They were using dogs on us, big savage ones. The very thought of it cranked our trouble-scale up another notch. Being tracked down by dogs is different than being hunted by choppers and other people. It makes you feel a sort of desperation whenever you think about it. Every creak of a branch in the wind becomes the bark you're half-expecting all the time. Whenever we were separated from each other we were even more worried.

We made it our policy to keep out of the huts as much as possible, checking them out for supplies and moving on to camp in a different place. "Like a couple of old boars chucked out of the mob," Uncle Hec remarked.

We packed a load of stuff into Broken-foot Camp. Our little whare was still there and everything was just as we'd stashed it. We stripped all the dried-up thatching off the roof, retied the poles with nylon cord and re-covered it with a sheet of polythene we carried from Cave Camp. Then we put down another layer of ferns, laid poles to hold it all down and it was cosier than ever. It was like coming home.

It was still too early for the possum skins to be at their best, but they were coming right, Uncle Hec said. "Still a bit of mating-damage on this one. We might have to give 'em a week or two yet."

We spent our time packing supplies from everywhere within reach of Broken-foot. We had no intention of going hungry this time. We collected a line of traps that someone had sprung and left over in the Whakatane Valley. They were very rusty, but most of them still worked. We pulled the rusting staples out of the trees with a sharpening-steel and packed the traps back to Broken-foot, thirty-three of them. We collected every nail and staple we could lever out of the walls of the huts, and took all the string and rope and wire and sacking and plastic — everything we could find, and lumped it all over to Broken-foot.

We were busy round the camp for a few days, and by the time we were ready to start trapping we had everything ready for the winter. Our food was stored in two wooden boxes between the bunks with a candle in a tin on the top for reading in bed. The main stash of supplies remained under a rock across the bush flat, buried in plastic bags and tins. Sacks were useful. They provided the floor and the door, and made good mattresses when stuffed with ferns on our bunks. Our spare clothes were stored under Uncle Hec's bunk and our packs and dry firewood under mine. We even had a calendar from two years before hanging on the wall. It had a cow standing in a swamp on it.

The slasher-head we'd found the year before was one of the most useful things around. We'd put a short kanuka handle in it and sharpened it with a file Robby had given us. We cut all our pungas and ferns and light stuff with it. The flat back edge was our hammer and the broad end of the blade was the best thing we had to dig with. One of the worst offences around Broken-foot was hitting a rock and blunting the slasher.

≈

And of course we had the radio. We couldn't get reception at Broken-foot in the daytime — too many hills in the way I suppose — but at night we could nearly always get the National Programme. This suited Uncle Hec all right, but the music they played was always yukky. We didn't hear ourselves mentioned on the news again, even after the police dog episode, but we reckoned it was more likely to have been on the local station and we couldn't receive that where we were. No news was good news as far as we were concerned.

"How come everyone gets us wrong all the time, Uncle Hec?" I asked him one night when we were sitting down looking into the fire.

"What do you mean?"

"Well every single time we have anything to do with other people we get into more trouble."

"What about Robby, and Quiet Brian? They don't give us any trouble."

"Yes they do," I said.

"How do you make that out?"

"We can't stay near them or *they'll* get into trouble, and that means more trouble for us. But I mean those rangers, and the police, and the

Social Welfare — why can't we get them to leave us alone?"

"They can't afford to leave us alone."

"But why?"

"Because if they let us get away with living in here they'd have to let anyone else who wants to, and most of 'em couldn't handle it. They'd get themselves straight into trouble and have to be rescued. Some of them'd get lost and die — the police can't afford to let it happen. They'd be mad if they did."

"You mean you *agree* with them?"

Uncle Hec loaded two more hunks of matai branch onto the fire.

"The police and me've got nothin' against one another," he said. "We just don't agree how to go about things, that's all."

"But the more we try to keep away from them, the harder they chase us," I said. "Not just the police, either. All of them. It's not fair. You're the only one I can trust out of everyone."

He looked at me and said, "You don't want to go trusting people, mate. You'll only disappoint yourself if you do that."

Then he mucked around with the fire a bit and said, "Now shut up, will you. I'm trying to listen to the wireless."

Hard to talk to sometimes, Uncle Hec. In fact we hardly ever talked these days, since we'd got the radio.

At last Uncle Hec pronounced that the skins weren't going to get much better than the ones we were catching around the camp for the dogs. They were very black and shiny, those furs, and I could see what he meant when he said they were unusually good ones.

We set our thirty-three traps up a ridge to the top and down another one, with long spaces between each trap so they could be shifted if they didn't catch. We put them on runs and against trees and roots and on logs — wherever we found a good set and plenty of possum-sign. We couldn't afford flour to bait our sets so we used little scraps of white paper to attract them, which Uncle Hec said was as good as anything where the possums hadn't been trapped before. Uncle Hec could set the traps with his hands but I had to put my foot on them to push the springs down.

I couldn't wait to get out round the line next morning to see what we'd caught. Fifteen possums, two blue bush rats and two sprung traps. We stunned the possums, bled them and hung them up near the trap. Eight of them had real good skins, so Uncle Hec was pleased.

Next day we got eight more good skins, skinned the ones from the day before and stretched the skins over pieces of driftwood and dead branch about as thick as your leg, if you've got thin legs, like me. We hung them under a skin-shelter on wires strung between two trees and soon we had fifty of them in there. They all had to be opened out and scraped and shaken loose and hung in bundles. Uncle Hec was fussy about how we prepared the skins, and we only took the very best of them.

In spite of several patches of dirty weather and having to shift the traps around all the time to keep them catching, we ended up after six weeks with 288 dried, scraped, pressed and bundled skins.

"Could be one of the best lines of skins I've seen," admitted Uncle Hec.

We were low on food by this time because we'd been doing a lot of eating and not much hunting, so we stashed everything and humped our packs over to Maungapohatu on our way down to Cave Camp and Robby's sheep station.

Next day we climbed up onto the Huiarau Range. We knew it had been snowing up here and the snow was still lying around in big patches. In the distance it had looked as bright and clean as manuka flowers after rain, but close up it was slushy and wet with a crusty sound when you walked in it. Black pools of water lay in the hollows along the ridge, reflecting the tree-tops and the sky. There was not a sound except the scrunching of our feet on the saturated ground. They were good conditions for pretending to be fur-trappers, making our way across the frozen wastes to the trading post at Hudson Bay.

We hadn't seen a single other person since we'd left Robby three months before.

CHAPTER
NINE

SIX
MONTHS

We arrived at Cave Camp in the afternoon and stayed the night there. We'd come a long way and waited a long time to get to Robby and we were looking forward to seeing him, but now that he was just a thousand feet down the ridge from us we weren't in any hurry. Our biggest worry wasn't whether he was still there, but whether he was still the same, still our friend. When you don't see any other people for a long time you start to wonder if what you remember about them is right. It makes you a bit nervous about seeing them again.

We heard someone banging something down at the station next day, and that night we sneaked down and gave our whistle for Robby which set his dogs barking. He was there, and judging by the way he greeted us you'd think he hadn't seen any other people either.

Robby said he'd been thinking about us for the past two days. "You skinny pair of bush rats," he said, pouring us a cup of tea, not knowing that there's no such thing as skinny when you've been a fat person.

We had a clean-up and sat round the table reading the news-paper cuttings Robby had saved for us. Then we ate a huge feed, including everything green he had in the place. Uncle Hec and I had been seen in several places during the winter, including the Ruahine Ranges, 300 kilometres to the south. But the main news was that the firearms charge against Uncle Hec had been reduced to one of behaving in a threatening manner, owing to "discrepancies in the statements of Bremner, Houghton and Drew", the rangers who'd caught us at Te Waiotukapiti. Our old friend, Sergeant Bowling, was quoted as saying that the police were no longer actively searching for Faulkner and Baker. It was unlikely that they were still in the bush and were probably being sheltered by accomplices somewhere in the back country. Faulkner was still wanted for questioning in connection with a number of offences and a general watch was being kept for the pair. They should still be approached with caution.

"It looks like they've given up on you," said Robby.

"Wouldn't get too carried away with that idea," said Uncle Hec.

We talked until after midnight that night. Robby had some good news. He'd been as good as told that if he applied for the managership of the station he'd get the job.

"I know I can make the place pay," he said. "But what about you blokes?"

"What about us?" said Uncle Hec.

"When do you turn fifteen, Ricky?"

"Six and a half months," I told him. "And four days."

"Have you thought what you're going to do after that?"

"No," I said. "Not really."

"We'll take care of that when we come to it," Uncle Hec said. "Ricky'll be all right. They won't be able to do much to him."

"What about you?"

"Don't worry about me. I'll be able to keep out of their way for a while yet."

"What do you reckon'd happen if you went out and gave yourselves up?" said Robby.

"Forget it."

"No, seriously. What do you reckon you'd get?"

"Hard to say. A man'd be lookin' at six months in the slammer, I'd reckon. At the least. As well as a lot of other hassles."

"Ricky could stay here until you got out, but you mightn't necessarily *get* locked up."

"You want to bet?"

"I've seen a lawyer about your case. A friend of mine."

Uncle Hec and I both jumped up from the table.

"You what!" I said.

"You bastard!" said Uncle Hec.

"Settle down," said Robby. "He'd lose his licence to practise if he told anyone else about it."

"Does he know we're here?" demanded Uncle Hec.

"He doesn't know where you are, and he wouldn't turn you in if he did."

"What did the lawyer say?" I asked him.

"He's pretty sure he can get the abduction charge dropped on a technicality. You were never properly served with the warrant in the first place. He thinks that's why they had to withdraw the reward officially for your apprehension."

"What about the other charge?" I asked.

"It all depends whether the rifle was loaded or not. If it wasn't and Hec says he was only trying to bluff them, there's a good chance of him being able to get them to reduce the charge even further. You could get off with a suspended sentence, Hec."

"What if they don't suspend it?" I asked.

"Six months," said Robby. "Something like that."

"Was it loaded, Uncle Hec?"

"Mind your own bloody business," he said.

"Even if you *said* it wasn't loaded," said Robby.

But Uncle Hec said, "Nice of you to try, mate, but I think I'll just hang on and see what turns up."

"Okay," said Robby, sighing. "It's your decision. But you ought to give it a bit of thought."

"Okay," said Uncle Hec. "We'll think about it."

Robby was due to go into town anyway, so the next day he took our skins in to sell and to get us some supplies we wanted. As it was the first money I'd ever actually earned myself I asked him to buy me a book about photography because I still wanted to give it a go. While Robby was gone I tried to talk to Uncle Hec about the idea of our giving ourselves up, but he was being difficult. I read a book while he cleared a drain at the side of the house. We had a meal cooking when Robby arrived back with all our stuff and more we hadn't asked for. He'd got 2764 dollars for our skins.

"They'll take as many skins like that as I can get them" said Robby. "They're the best that's come in this season."

He'd brought my book, *Photography for Beginners*. I had almost memorised it by the time I went to sleep that night.

We couldn't stay with Robby. Some valuers were due to start working there any day, so we made arrangements to come again in a few weeks. If the doors at the top of the woolshed ramp were open it would be safe to come down. We loaded our packs, untied the dogs and said goodbye to Robby and left for Cave Camp. The next day we left on a trip over to the western side of the Urewera.

≈

Every time we travelled out along the Kotare Ridge our situation had changed, and it was different again this time. The reward for our apprehension had been officially withdrawn, and if the police weren't seriously looking for us, other people weren't likely to bother. We weren't news any more, and the worst they could do to us was stick Uncle Hec in the "slammer" for a few months and me in a Social Welfare home. The main change this time was that the seriousness had gone out of our situation, and that was important, but it was nothing to the changes waiting for us over in the Whakatane Valley.

We found we could use the tracks and huts like anyone else. In fact it seemed as though we had the whole area to ourselves. It was a week before we ran into anyone at all. But the less we avoided them the more they seemed to avoid us. We found two hunters in the Parahaki hut one night, and they were so nervous of us that they gave us some of their food and left in the rain for Central Waiau rather than spend the night in the same hut with us. Makes you feel as if there's something wrong with you, that sort of thing. And it got worse. Those people we did meet would get off the track and let us pass, glad to see us go. They didn't know if we were still supposed to be dangerous or not, I suppose, but it can certainly get to you, being approached with caution.

We arrived at Totara hut one day and when I grabbed the door handle to open it someone was holding it from the inside.

"Go away," a squeaky voice called out. "The hut's full. There's no room. You'll have to go away!"

Uncle Hec and I looked at each other and left the poor bloke there on his own and went on to Skipper's hut.

Just after that we passed a bunch of people on the Lake Track and I heard an overweight lady say, "They're filthy!"

"We're thin though," I yelled back at her.

Fat people don't forget things like that.

We tried to swap a leg of pork for a loaf of bread with some people living in a bus at the edge of the Galatea side, but they were vegetarians. A chopper landed near us in a clearing one day and we went over for a chat with them, but when we were halfway there they took off again. I found myself half-hoping we'd meet up with people on every track, so we could find out how we stood with them.

Then we had a stroke of terrible luck. We were on a leading ridge, heading over to Te Raki to pick up a stash of food we had there, and the dogs found this boar on the top of the ridge and ran it right down to the creek and started bailing hard on it.

"Sounds like they're settled in down there," said Uncle Hec. "We'll have to go and give them a hand."

So we dropped our packs and slid and groped our way through the supplejack and steep roots, guided by the frantic barking. When we arrived they had the pig down in an almost-dry creek with three-metre sides like a ditch. The boar, a big one, was backed in against the bank. It was black and white and hairy, with half of its face white and the other half black, which made it look more dangerous. Its hackles were sticking up and you could hear its tusks working on its grinders from where we were at the top of the bank. It made a high skreaking noise.

"Doesn't look too good to me," said Uncle Hec. The angle's wrong. Don't know if I can drop him from here."

Just then the boar charged the dogs and they had to go for their lives down the creek bed. The pig ran back to his spot and bailed up there, facing the dogs.

"We'll have to give it a go. He's going to get one of the dogs in a minute."

He leant the rifle across a small tree at the top of the bank, *crack* — and the pig went down on its front knees and the dogs moved in and started tearing at its head and neck. Then the boar stood up and flicked Zag into the air, rammed Willy against the bank and started ripping into him. I just had to stand and watch. Willy was a helpless yowling mess of blood, with Zag hopelessly tugging at one of the boar's back legs. Uncle Hec kept shooting — *crack* — *crack* — *crack* — and not making any difference either. Another *crack*, and he got it. The boar fell kicking in the mud it had churned up. Uncle Hec went straight over the bank and dragged the bucking carcase with Zag still tugging at it away from Willy, who was trying to get up on his front feet. Uncle Hec knifed the boar, and I was down there lifting Willy away from the foot of the bank. I remember every stone in that bank. He was covered with blood and it was hard to tell exactly where he'd been ripped, but there was a lot of flesh hanging down one side of this neck.

Uncle Hec reached past me and lifted Willy's head.

"He's had it, Ricky. You'd better get out of here. I might have to finish him off."

"But can't we . . ."

"*Take off, Ricky!*"

You don't argue with him when he talks like that. I stepped over the dead boar without looking at it again and went down the creek until I found a place to climb out and trudge back to the packs on the ridge. A bit later Uncle Hec arrived. He put his hand on my shoulder.

"Sorry about that, Ricky," he said, still breathing heavily. "I just couldn't get a decent shot at that pig. He killed Willy. He was dead before you were out of sight. His neck was broke. I pulled some rocks down on him. Good dog that. Turned out all right."

"I hate bloody pigs," I said, and I meant it. They'd killed my dog. My Willy.

"I know how you feel, mate. I've lost a few like that."

"How are we going to manage with only one dog?"

"We'll have to find out. We'd better hope we don't run into any more boars like that one. Zag's getting a bit slow for that kind of pig."

I wasn't very pleased with life after that, but three nights after Willy's death an important thing happened by accident. A talk with Uncle Hec.

We'd got mucked up on a ridge and ended up camped in a deep gorge with the Te Hoe River roaring past a few yards away. There was a log-jamb there and we built up a big fire to make up for not having enough to eat. It was a drastic place — wild. We were sitting on a log drying our sleeping-bags and I wanted to ask him something.

"Uncle Hec?" I said.

"Look, Ricky," he said. "There's no need to call me uncle all the time. We both know I'm your uncle. I don't call you nephew all the time, do I?"

"It's all right, Uncle Hec," I told him. "I know you don't like me. But don't you worry, as soon as I'm fifteen I'll be off your hands and you'll never have to see me ever again if you don't want to." And I don't know how it happened but all of a sudden I was crying. Right there in front of him. Bawling my eyes out. Couldn't help it.

Then Uncle Hec went and reached out and grabbed me by the shoulder of the shirt and dragged me right up against him where he was sitting and held me there with his arm round me. Right up against him without either of us looking away from the fire.

"Come on, old mate," he said. "I know you've had a rough trot, but you can handle it."

Well, him saying something like that, and giving me a bit of a squeeze as well, must have been too much for me. I blubbered my stupid head off. Told him a few things, too. Personal stuff about him and me and the way he treated me. Things he'd done and said. Unfair stuff. And I told him about my dog. My Willy. The only thing I ever had of my own and killed by that black-and-white boar in the Te Raki. Uncle Hec didn't say anything.

When all the crying was gone we sat there for a while, just looking at the fire and hearing the river roaring past out there in the dark. Then he said, "You want to hear my side of it?"

I wiped my face on my sleeve, looked up and nodded.

"When Bella died like that I didn't care much what the hell happened. I didn't want to see you stuck in a home, but there was nothin' I could do about it. I certainly couldn't be bothered arguing with you about it. You can be a stubborn little bastard when you want to be.

"So I made up my mind to take you into the bush and give you a hard time so you'd want to chuck it in. Then you'd be off my hands. That's why I made you walk so far that first day. There are two huts closer to the farm than Mangatoatoa."

"Is that why you don't like us going over that way?" I said. "Scared I'll find out?"

"Shut up. I didn't think you'd be able to handle it, but I've been stuck with you ever since."

"Stuck with me? How?"

"I'd made up my mind to keep it up till you couldn't take it any more and would want to quit. But you still haven't quit. You're a stubborn coot all right."

"Do you mean if I said I'd wanted to quit you *would* have?"

"Yeah. Any time. I'd've had to."

"What were you going to do?"

"I don't know. Trot you out and turn you in at the nearest Social Welfare office, I suppose."

"Well you don't *have* to put up with me," I told him. "You can hand me over to them whenever you like."

He reached out and shook the end of a log that was sticking out of the fire and the whole thing collapsed inwards in a shower of sparks and flame. "You're not very smart sometimes, are you, mate?" he said.

"What do you mean?"

"You seem to think a man'd be stupid enough to go through all this with someone he wants to get rid of. I'm proud a y', mate. Y' got more guts than I ever gave y' credit for."

"Well I don't know unless you tell me, do I? You never tell me anything. I can't even tell if you want me around or not."

"Forgetting something, aren't you, Ricky?"

"What?"

"We're related, mate. Same family, remember?"

When Uncle Hec said that to me nothing else he'd said or done mattered. It was the first time I'd ever had a relative who admitted it straight out, and who was proud of me as well. We liked each other a bit better after that, and Uncle Hec treated me more equally. We got onto fewer wrong ridges.

As a matter of fact I tried out calling him Hec one day. It was his turn walking in front with the rifle and we were splashing along down an easy creek into the Whakatane, and I said, "How far is it out to the river, Hec?"

"An hour and a bit," he said over his shoulder.

When he got to the next crossing he stopped and looked round at me, and when he turned back and splashed into the crossing he was just starting to grin. I saw him.

Glad you didn't look round again after that, Uncle Hec. I was too pleased just then to have anyone looking at me.

≈

We ran into a few more people on the tracks and round the huts and they all treated us as if we had AIDS. But one day something really funny happened. We were bowling along the Te Wai-iti Track and ran into our good friend Hugh the Park Board ranger and another bloke.

They stopped when they saw us coming and hurried back the way they'd come. Uncle Hec and I grinned at each other and trotted after them. We found where their marks left the track and we chased them through the bush making just enough noise to let them know they were being followed. They were too scared even to split up.

After a few hundred yards of this Zag showed us where they were both hiding up a tree. We stood there and looked at them. Hugh dropped his big rifle with the telescopic sights and it fell down the hill and slid out of sight among the leaves. His mate didn't have one.

"I stuck up for you guys!" Hugh called out.

We didn't say anything. We just went away and left them there. I like the way Uncle Hec does things sometimes. Kind of neat.

CHAPTER
TEN

OKAY

We were sitting by one of our big fires in the open at Hanamahihi, and there was something Uncle Hec had been avoiding.

"We have to make a decision about that stuff Robby was talking about," I said. "About us staying in the bush or giving ourselves up. We have to decide, Uncle Hec."

"We couldn't decide at Robby's place," he said.

"Why not?"

"We've got something else to decide about first, and it wasn't the right time."

"When's the right time?"

"Now'd be as good as any."

"What is it?"

He mucked around with the fire a bit and then sat back on the chunk of beech he was using for a seat. I could always tell when he had something special to say.

"You remember those kokako we came across on the Huiarau that day the choppers were chasing us. Those birds we found?"

I remembered it. We'd had to keep off the ridges and we'd just seen them drop someone off about half a mile ahead of us. Going back was too risky, so we dropped off the Huiarau Range in a tricky place and sidled round some bluffs. We came to a little clearing where a tree had fallen and Uncle Hec stopped and waved me to come up quietly.

"Look," he whispered. "See that bird?"

A big shiny bird with an orange tuft on its neck was hopping around in the branches of a dead beech tree, picking grubs out of the peeling bark. Another one, a bit smaller with a smaller, straighter beak and not so brilliant, flew in and hopped and skipped up the same branch.

"What . . . ?" I whispered.

"Shut up."

So we watched these big black birds jumping around in the tree until another one, blue-black in the sunlight, glided in and joined them. Then another one arrived. Four big birds, two pairs it looked like, hopping around in this dead tree making high and low whistling noises and some strange clucking sounds.

We really should have been moving on — there was an army chopper working just along from us.

"What are they?" I whispered.

"Kokako."

"Kokako?"

"Yeah, a kind of native parrot. They're pretty scarce. If you can prove there's kokako in a block you can stop 'em milling the timber."

I don't think they heard us whispering, but one of the birds gave a loud whistle and glided right past us, so close we could hear the air whistling through its feathers. Then the others, one two three, dropped out of the dead beech and glided past us and out of sight through the bush.

"Do you reckon you could find this place again?" asked Uncle Hec.

"Yeah, sure," I said. "We'd better move, hadn't we? We'll get caught, standing around here."

"This exact spot. That tree there," he insisted.

"Sure," I said. "You just come over the side of the Huiarau out of that pepperwood saddle and sidle down till you come to that grove of tawhara. You have to come round above that slip and stay at the same level till you come to these bluffs."

"Okay," he said, "but what if we had to find it from the other direction? Could you find it if we came in from that ridge over there?"

"I could once we've been that way. Let's go, eh."

"How sure are you?"

"Sure as I can be. Let's *go*."

So we went. Uncle Hec kept looking around for landmarks, but I think he must have been taking his bearings off the clouds because when we looked back from the next ridge, he picked out the wrong bluffs.

≈

Yes, I remembered the kokako. Better than Uncle Hec did probably.

"What about them?" I said.

"They weren't kokako."

"What were they then?"

He exploded the fire with a kick.

"I'm pretty sure they're huia," he said.

"Huia?"

"Yeah. They're supposed to have died out years ago. Those must be the only ones left alive."

"That makes it a pretty important discovery, doesn't it?"

"More than I can imagine, and I've been thinkin' about it."

"Why didn't you tell me before?"

"Had to make up me mind whether I was going t' tell you at all."

"Why?"

"We were attracting a fair bit of attention as it was that day, but it's nothing to the attention you'll get when they find out you've discovered an extinct bird. It'll be news all over the bloody world."

"What shall we do?"

"Might pay us to make sure before we go too much further. I'd like to get another look at those birds. D'you reckon you could find that place again?"

"Kokako Bluffs? Sure," I said. I wasn't exactly sure, but I wasn't letting on to Uncle Hec.

We got up onto the Huiarau next day and Uncle Hec led the expedition. I don't know if he could have found Kokako Bluffs again if it wasn't for me. He went the wrong way three times and would have ended up hundreds of feet too low on the face of the range. He was bad-tempered with embarrassment by the time we came to the bluffs, right near where I'd been telling him they were.

We were still a quarter of a mile or so from where we'd seen the birds the first time when we heard them again — low clear whistles, some very high ones, and then some clucking sounds. They were skipping around in the branches of a miro tree this time. Only one pair of them. The female was very bright and shiny, blue-black, the male smaller and duller. They had orange tufts at their throats.

We watched them for about an hour, following them when they flew off to another tree. They were very tame and easy to get close to — especially for us.

"That's huias all right," whispered Uncle Hec. "I'm bloody sure of it."

"Are you absolutely certain?"

"Certain as I can be. There's nothin' else I know of looks anything like 'em. Look at that white on the end of their tails. The Maoris used to use them feathers for decorations. There's nothin' else they could be."

I had a feeling he was right. "Let's get away from here and work out what we're going to do about it," I said. "We've got to get out of this place yet."

Getting out of that place was easier said than done. We'd been lucky the time before, and desperate. We couldn't go back up onto the ridge because we'd slid down shingle, and we tried two other routes but got into trouble both times. In the finish I had to drop Zag over a fifteen-foot ledge and Uncle Hec caught him and threw him across a split in the rock and we climbed down a tree onto the easier slope below the bluffs. We had to make the last bit to the Huiarau hut that night with a candle in a tin.

I want to say right here that I regard Uncle Hec as the discoverer of the huias. He saw them first and it was he who identified them. Besides, no one but Uncle Hec would have ever dropped over the side of the Huiarau Range in a place like that. You could say it was the fruits of his unique bushmanship, but he kept talking as though I was the one who'd made the discovery and he was just tagging along. I didn't wake up to him at first.

"I reckon I could get photographs of those huias," I said.

"You reckon?"

"I reckon."

"If you could do that — I don't know what they'd be worth, but it'd be thousands of dollars."

"Thousands of dollars?"

"Hundreds of thousands, probably. Enough to set you up with whatever you wanted. You know what huiarau means?"

"No, what?"

"Huia-rau. Rau means a hundred, a hundred huias. There must have been plenty of them round there in the early days. There'll be one hell of a stink when they find out there's still some left."

"What do you think we should do about it?" I asked.

"I don't really want anything to do with it," he said.

"But, Uncle Hec, it's an important discovery."

"Yeah, I know. But I couldn't handle all the publicity and stuff. I'm too old for that sort of caper. Why don't you get into it? You like birds, don't you?"

"What about Robby's idea of our giving ourselves up?" I said. "We still haven't talked about that yet."

"Haven't we?"

"No. Someone keeps putting it off. We've got to decide about that sooner or later, Uncle Hec, but you just won't talk about it."

"How long is it now until you're fifteen?"

"Five months and one week," I told him. "And six days."

"You'd probably be all right then," he said. "It'll take them about that long to sort out what to do with you."

"What about you?" I said.

"I'll be okay. They won't catch me."

I'd been scared he was going to be like this.

"We mightn't even get locked up. Robby said it all depends if the rifle was loaded or not."

"That's what he reckons."

"Was it loaded, Uncle Hec? We could always say it wasn't anyway, but *was* it?"

He shrugged. "You know that as well as I do."

"No I don't," I said. "Stop mucking around, Uncle Hec. This is important. Was it loaded or not?"

He did something unnecessary to the fire and then he said, "Who was carrying the rifle when we first got to that hut?"

" . . . Me."

"Who unloaded it?"

"I did."

"What did you do with the bullets?"

"They were in my pocket."

"Where was the rest of the ammunition?"

"In the plastic bag in the bottom of my pack — Uncle Hec! You didn't even have any bullets in the rifle! You're a great actor!"

"It would have been loaded if I could have," he grumbled. "And I'd've used it if I'd had to."

"That's not the point. We can prove it *wasn't* loaded. You mightn't have to go to jail at all. Robby's lawyer said so."

"Who's going to listen to us? No, mate, if we stick our heads out there we're lookin' at gettin' locked up. You're kiddin' yourself if you think any different."

That's where you leave it for later with Uncle Hec. The conversation goes flat if you push him beyond this stage, if you know what I mean.

≈

We camped in the Ohaua hut the next night, but Uncle Hec's foot was giving him trouble. It was the night after that, camped in the Kakewahine streambed, that I brought the subject up again. There was nothing you could hear properly on the radio, the fire was one of our big ones and we were sitting back from it with our backs against a rimu log. It was a still dark night, not a star in sight. The moreporks seemed to think it was going to rain so we had our sheet of black polythene out ready. The loudest noise came from a lump of totara sparking and cracking in the fire. It was as good a time as any. He'd said something humorous that afternoon, which was a good sign.

"I quit, Uncle Hec," I said to him.

"What are you talking about?"

"I want to quit. I've had enough. I want to get out of the bush."

He looked at me with his face turned off.

"You're no quitter," he said. "What's brought this on?"

"I just don't want to stay in the bush any more. I want to chuck it in."

"What about the Social Welfare? I thought you were scared of that crowd."

"I can handle it," I said. "It's only a few months, and I'm thin now."

"What the hell's that got to do with it?"

"Lots," I told him. "Come on, how about it, Uncle Hec?"

"They'll probably stick you in a home till you're fifteen."

"They might, but that's nothing. You might have to spend the same time in jail. It's the least time we'd have to be split up, this way. Please, Uncle Hec. We've gone through all this together, we've got to stick together now."

"I'm not going out there and giving myself up to them drongoes. You can forget it. I'll think about it again when you're fifteen."

"But that's when we can be free. After that we can sell photographs of the huias and go anywhere and do anything we like. You said so yourself. Please, Uncle Hec! If we don't do it this way it's going to be a *whole year*!"

"Nar."

"Forgetting something, aren't you, Uncle Hec?" I said.

"What's that?"

"We're related, mate. Same family, remember?"

He got up and poked around with the fire and stayed standing, lit from behind in the firelight he'd stirred up.

"Okay. If that's the way you want it. After this little lot a few months in the slammer'd be a picnic. I've never had such a gutful of the bush in me bloody life."

It was a little while before I could talk after he said that. Our most important decision had been brought out in the open at last. And it had been made, resolved. It was as if all the things that had happened to us made sense now. Our lives were going somewhere. Together.

There are some things you know about but you don't like to test them in case they turn out not to be true. The big question that had been hanging between Uncle Hec and me was what we were going to do when I turned fifteen. Each of us had been scared the other wouldn't want us to stay together. Now we both knew we did.

"You know what, Uncle Hec?" I said to him.

"What?"

"I'm not the only stubborn bastard around here."

He looks real nice when he smiles.

With all that out of the way all we had to do was to eat and make plans. The bush was different again. We were going to leave the Urewera. There was a limit to it. We decided that until I could get skilled and take some photographs of the huias we'd keep our discovery to ourselves. No one would believe us anyway, without proof. We reckoned that if we released one good colour photo of a pair of supposedly extinct huias through an agent — possibly Robby's lawyer friend — we mightn't ever have to go near them again, and they'd be protected from conservationists and bird-lovers and rangers and naturalists and all their other friends.

"If they couldn't find us in here, there's not much chance of them finding a handful of birds," said Uncle Hec.

Meantime the huias were up our sleeve, our trump card, our

back-stop — perhaps even our future. It was a good feeling that made our other hassles seem less significant. But the main thing about it all was still me and Uncle Hec. After all, we were family, and that's the most important thing. We were sticking together.

We told Robby about our decision to give ourselves up when we next visited, but we didn't say anything about the huias. We mightn't ever be able to find them again, as far as we knew, and it was better to keep it under our hats for the time being. He was very anxious to help us in any way he could, but we didn't want him doing too much. It was our hassle — family business.

We had 1800 dollars left with Robby from our possum skins. Uncle Hec asked him to look after Zag for us and we left the .22 with him too, in case it got confiscated. He gave us the name and address of his lawyer but we lost it somewhere and all I could remember when we got back into the bush was that his name was Charles.

"Whatever happens to us out there, we meet back here," I reminded Uncle Hec in front of Robby.

And they both agreed.

≈

Robby had actually been saving supplies for us, most of which we had to leave behind. This time when we travelled the Kotare Ridge into the Urewera things were different again. It was the end of something we'd lived, and the beginning of something new. Walking along behind Uncle Hec with no rifle, no dogs and no need to watch out for other people, I got into remembering it all.

I remembered back down three thousand kilometres of bush tracks to the little farm at Apopo. I remembered Aunty Bella and the big feeds and her ruffling my hair and calling me lamb — there was always a bit of sadness there. Then the hunting and getting my own dog, Willy. Then the funeral and Uncle Hec and I deciding to hide out in the bush till I was fifteen. The big grey boar looking at me in the creek at Kahikatea . . . scrounging around the huts for food. The smell of the sun on hot rock at Broken-foot, and Uncle Hec hobbling around with his foot, and me worrying about getting us enough to eat. Carrying the stag out of Blue-sow Creek . . . and the Bird-lady, gone back to her tribe on the Limmin River in Arnhem Land.

Finding the poster in the Tauwharana hut saying we were wanted by the police . . . the sick ranger in the Koranga Forks hut . . . Quiet Brian, friendliness and possum fat. Then the rangers in the Te Waiotukapiti hut, and Uncle Hec standing out there in the mist by the woodblock with no bullets in the rifle, telling them they wouldn't get hurt if they didn't interfere with us. I got so carried away when I remembered about that I couldn't help reaching forward and touching Uncle Hec on the back of the arm.

"What are you doin'?" he said.

"Nothing, Uncle Hec."

"Keep back a bit, will y'. You'll trip a man up."

"Okay."

Then the big search for us . . . dodging the searchers and choppers and dogs through the bush. We'd been lucky a lot of times. Then Cave Camp, and Robby, and discovering I was thin in Robby's bathroom mirror. The police dog and the big fight with Willy and Zag at Te Pourewa . . . trapping the possums at Broken-foot . . . the radio hanging in a konini tree, telling us we'd been seen by trampers over beyond Lake Waikaremoana . . . the big ugly black-and-white boar that killed my dog in the dry creek at Te Raki. My Willy.

All our old camps and the places we'd given names to. The

constant scrounging and hunting and hoping for food. The times we were so hungry we could only think about finding an animal with our dogs, to kill it and take its meat and eat it. And underneath all that was the underlying feeling of us having discovered the huias and what it might mean in our lives. It was hard to fit it all into nineteen months in my mind, but that's how long Uncle Hec and I had lasted it out in the bush. Nineteen months.

We came in here with nothing, and now we were going out with a good chance of being able to have anything we could think of and go anywhere we liked, without being interfered with by other people. But there was more to it than that — I'd learnt something from the bush.

The Urewera country had taken things off me and given me things. It had sheltered me and frightened me. The bush still stands there growing and minding its own business. The ridges are just as high and broken as they ever were. The streams and rivers still tumble and rush and flood down the valleys. The rain and snow and sun and wind still please themselves what they do without being interested in me. But I see it differently now.

It'd taught me something other people never could. It'd taught me how to stick to rules that weren't my rules, just like everything else had to. In fact I was beginning to see how it all works. The rock gives in to the vegetable kingdom. The vegetable world takes from the mineral and gives up itself to the animal world. And then me, human beings, people — the last in the whole arrangement. But I could only take advantage of my place in it by sticking to the rules, and to step out of line could get me killed. It taught you respect, realising a thing like that. It might be the same with everything, for all I know, and just go on forever.

≈

We hung around a few of our favourite places until there was really nothing left to talk about. We were more like two people going on holiday than a pair of bush rats wanted by the police, going out to give themselves up.

"You'll have to do most of the talking," said Uncle Hec. "I'd only end up flattenin' somebody. Do you reckon you can handle it?"

"Sure," I said. "I can handle it."

"You'd better, you skinny young coot, or I'll flatten you for a start."

"If you ruffle my hair like that again, Hec," I said, "I'll stick you across my knee and flatten your backside."

And we shoved each other around a bit in the sand in front of the fire.

He does look nice when he smiles.

≈

The day after that there was nothing else to do. We slid down a bank onto the Waikaremoana road and stuck our thumbs out when we heard the venison truck coming up behind us.

≈

We've got a few hassles coming up, but we can handle them. We're okay now.

CHAPTER
ELEVEN

EPITAPH

'm Robby Barton, Hec and Ricky's friend, and I feel impelled to add what I know to Ricky's story.

The first I saw of Hec and Ricky was some smoke up on the bluffs at the back of the station. Then I saw Ricky and his dogs one day. I guessed they were the ones the big search was on for when they stayed there for so long, and when the hue and cry had died down I rode up there, found their camp, and waited.

Their camp was a mouldy nest of ponga-fronds under an overhang of rock, albeit rather cunningly concealed, and their few pathetic possessions were hidden under some pulled fern. Their sleeping-bags were disgusting.

They appeared suddenly from among the rocks, from where they must have been watching me, and it was all I could do to keep the shock off my face. They were both dressed in rags tied around them with strips of torn cloth and flax. Where a button was missing they'd poked the cloth through the button-hole and inserted a piece of stick through it. One of the boy's trouser-legs had frayed off above the knee and the leg was covered with old bruises and scratches and he had a large scab on his knee that didn't look at all healthy.

Similarly one of the old man's shirtsleeves was torn off at the shoulder; his arm was scratched and scarred and there was a filthy piece of rag tied around a deep graze on his wrist. Their boots were falling to pieces and by all rights should have crippled them.

The old man, Hec, was gaunt and stringy, with a straggly grey hacked-off beard and sunken piercing eyes. He had a pronounced limp, which I learned later was the result of an accident to his foot that had never healed properly.

The boy, Ricky, was a good-looking Maori chap. His hair stuck out in tufts from his head and his hands and face were streaked with inground dirt. There was something almost primitive-looking about him.

And they stank. Badly. Both of them.

The old man carried a battered old pea-rifle and they had two very thin dogs with them. They were both very nervous, especially the boy. They had a habit of glancing at one another every few seconds, for reassurance perhaps. One got the impression that the wrong word or action could put them into full flight at a moment's notice.

I talked to them for some minutes and assured them they were safe with me and invited them down to the homestead for a wash and a meal. I didn't know whether to expect them or not, but they arrived out of the dark that night like two wild animals, blinking in the light, looking around suspiciously and glancing quickly at each other at every sound. It was quite unnerving, to be honest.

I got some greens into them and they ate like animals. In fact I wasn't sure when they were going to stop eating. They even consumed the scraps I normally throw out to the fowls.

The boy, Ricky, discovered he was thin for the first time when he went to take a bath here. It was really quite touching. Evidently he was quite a plump lad when they'd gone into the bush more than a year earlier.

Their story was a simple one. Hec's wife, Ricky's aunt, had died suddenly. They'd taken to the bush to wait until Ricky was fifteen, so that he wouldn't have to go back into a welfare home, and they'd been hounded ever since. It was my opinion that the lad would have been better off in any sort of home, but they'd made up their minds and no thought of giving up their original resolution seemed to have occurred to them. One had to be very careful what one said, especially in front of Hec, and especially at first. He relaxed considerably on acquaintance, and so did Ricky.

They stayed with me here for about a fortnight, during which time I got them cleaned up and dressed and fed. They would have appeared perfectly normal, except that every unusual sound, and quite a few usual ones as well, would cause them to freeze, glance quickly at one another and look around for the nearest thing to hide behind.

They were pathetically anxious to help round the station. They were good workers and knew their way around the stock. Their dogs were remarkably obedient. All they needed was more time to adjust to normal living. Unfortunately they could think of nothing but going back into the bush. They left here just as winter was setting in, to trap some opossums they knew of over in the Ruakituri somewhere.

I was quite concerned about Hec and Ricky by this time. I consulted Charles Roper, a lawyer and friend of mine, about their case. He made a few discreet enquiries for me in legal and police circles, and the consensus of opinion was that Hec would be fortunate to get off with less than six months' imprisonment, but if he was co-operative a suspended sentence wasn't entirely out of the question. I couldn't imagine Hec co-operating with his pursuers.

It was three months before I saw them again. I was cooking my meal one evening when they came sneaking in through the yards with two bundles of opossum skins in sacks wrapped with vines. The clothes I'd sent them off in were hanging on them in greasy rags and they stank of sweat and opossum fat and a kind of wood-smoke smell they always had about them. They were as wild-eyed and suspicious as ever, but seemed to relax a little sooner than they had the first time. They hadn't seen another soul since they'd left here, which they regarded as great good fortune.

I made them have a bath and got them into clothes that didn't smell and fed them. There *are* limits. I sold their furs for them, over 2000 dollars' worth, and bought them some supplies they needed. They were both so hopeless with money that I opened an account with myself for them. They actually had more cash than I did at that time because that was before I was made manager here. My wife and the girls were still living in town at that stage and knew nothing about my strange visitors.

By this time the charges against Hec had been reduced to behaving in a threatening manner (due largely to a legal technicality), and abducting a minor. This charge was seen by many as legally flimsy. The reward for information leading to his arrest had been officially withdrawn and the police were obviously sick of the whole affair.

Hec and Ricky were actually less endangered than they themselves imagined. They were quite out of touch. I tried to point out that it was a good time for them to give themselves up, but they were determined to stick it out until Ricky was fifteen, which at this stage was in about six months. They were very stubborn, both of them.

They left here on some trip or other and three weeks later they arrived back, already filthy, and said that they'd decided to give themselves up to the police after all.

They were determined to be independent about the matter and wouldn't even let me contact Charles for them. They had to do it their own way. I gave them Charles's name and phone number, but I found it when I was airing their bedding after they'd gone again.

They'd lost one of their dogs and left their remaining one with me, a tough old header they called Zag. He was about twelve years old and they'd run the poor old fellow off his feet. He was exhausted; I couldn't put any condition on him and he died during that winter.

They also left their old Winchester .22 with me because they were afraid it might be confiscated. It's still here, that rifle. I run an oily rag over it sometimes when I'm cleaning my own gun. I wouldn't fire the thing, it's very worn and knocked about. I keep it as a reminder of those two, because I don't believe they'll ever be coming back to collect it.

When they went back into the bush I didn't hear any more of them until the story of their surrender to the police broke in the news. They were very anxious not to involve me and my name was never mentioned, even though I was with them through so much of the ensuing legalities and publicity that people couldn't help speculating on my role in it.

Ricky got his five months in a welfare home. Hec, after a much-publicised trial, got a nine-month suspended sentence, a 1000 dollar fine, and was put on a good-behaviour bond for two years. Honour was satisfied. Charles did a splendid job of defending him.

Hec gave me a hand on the station and came with me into town each week to visit Ricky until his time was up. They both adjusted quite admirably, but I could have sworn those two were fretting for each other. They only seemed to be completely comfortable when they were together.

In spite of his natural reserve, Ricky got to be something of a favourite in the home and he didn't seem to be particularly unhappy there. He was growing into a remarkably handsome lad, with a most engaging shy smile, fine teeth and large brown eyes. He was to all outward appearances settling into civilised life quite well, although during one visit, I did accidentally overhear Hec admonishing him not to attempt escaping from there. It went something along the lines of:

"But, Uncle Hec, I could get out of here any time I like now. They even let me go down to the shops!"

"You turn up out at Robby's one day before your time's up, and I'll bloody well flatten you!"

At which point I passed out of earshot.

The day we picked Ricky up from the home he and Hec did some shopping. They only had 600-odd dollars to their names, but they spent nearly all of it on photographic equipment. I was initially very pleased to see the boy developing an interest like that, but when I realised that they were planning another trip into the bush I became concerned. If anyone should have had enough of trips into the Urewera it was those two, but they seemed quite enthusiastic about it —just when I was beginning to believe they were returning to normal. I even had Hec looking quite respectable.

I couldn't talk them out of it. They had some implausible tale about wanting to photograph some of the places they'd seen in there. Ricky had been out of the home for less than a month, most of the time spent messing about with photography, when they packed their gear and left on "a short trip round a few of the huts".

That was two years ago now and I haven't seen them since. Nor has anybody else, so far as can be ascertained. When they'd been gone for three months I went into the Gisborne Police Station and reported them missing, somewhere in the Urewera. You may well imagine the response I got.

Many people are of the opinion, kept alive by occasional reported sightings, that Faulkner and Baker are still dodging around the huts in the Ureweras. They still get blamed for much of the mischief done in there. I never believed it. And since I found Ricky's story, written in visitors' books taken from the huts and wrapped in a torn piece of black polythene among the stuff they left here, I've formed my own theory about what happened to them.

It's taken me nearly all winter to unravel Ricky's handwriting and get his story written down more or less how he meant it. One of his books has been wet and one whole passage is indecipherable. I could tell, though, from a few phrases I was able to follow, that Hec and Ricky planned to buy this station and present it to me in return for my having helped them. Another piece I was able to pick out was Ricky saying to Hec, "Maori skin isn't so brown on thin people as fat ones. True. I tell you!"

One or two other things he's left out of his story, such as the scene I remember in the kitchen here when Ricky discovered that Hec was illiterate. And later the touching little scene when Hec told Ricky he could have the .22 on his fifteenth birthday.

I must say here that everything I knew about in Ricky's story was quite true, and consistent with what they'd both told me. As for the huia, I don't know, but Ricky's description of them tallies in all respects with every reference I can find to them. If I had to guess, I'd say that those huia still exist, and that Hec and Ricky found them.

Owen Mallory, who was here last summer with his team, practising for one of his Himalayan expeditions, described any attempt to tackle those Huiarau bluffs without the proper equipment and experience in rock-climbing as "extremely foolhardy".

And that's what I think must have happened to them. Hec and Ricky must have dropped off one more ridge in a tricky place — too tricky. I do believe they're still out there in the Urewera bush, two ragged skeletons lying at the bottom of some bluffs, somewhere along the Huiarau Range. Kokako Bluffs.

And yet if I walked outside right now and saw that wisp of

smoke I always look for up on Cave Camp Bluffs — but no, it's been too long now.

That's all I have to tell, except that whenever I notice their old rifle there in the corner I think of Hec and Ricky, and I recall those last few words of Ricky's story:

"We've got a few hassles coming up, but we can handle them. We're okay now."

I'm not a particularly religious man, but if there's any justice in this life Ricky and his Uncle Hec *are* okay. Still sticking it out together and handling their own hassles in their own way. I hope so.

HUNT FOR THE WILDERPEOPLE CREDITS

DEFENDER FILMS, PIKI FILMS AND CURIOUS
IN ASSOCIATION WITH
THE NEW ZEALAND FILM COMMISSION
AND NEW ZEALAND ON AIR

PRESENT A FILM BY TAIKA WAITITI

HUNT FOR THE WILDERPEOPLE

SAM NEILL
JULIAN DENNISON

RHYS DARBY
RIMA TE WIATA
RACHEL HOUSE
OSCAR KIGHTLEY
TIOREORE NGATAI-MELBOURNE
TROY KINGI
COHEN HOLLOWAY
STAN WALKER
MIKE MINOGUE
HAMISH PARKINSON
LLOYD SCOTT

CINEMATOGRAPHER LACHLAN MILNE
EDITORS LUKE HAIGH, THOMAS EAGLES,
YANA GORSKAYA
PRODUCTION DESIGNER NEVILLE
STEVENSON
COSTUME DESIGNER KRISTIN SETH
MAKEUP DESIGNER DANNELLE SATHERLEY
CASTING DIRECTOR STUART TURNER
ORIGINAL SCORE BY LUKE BUDA, SAMUEL
SCOTT & CONRAD WEDDE
EXECUTIVE PRODUCERS JAMES WALLACE,
CHARLIE MCCLELLAN
PRODUCED BY CARTHEW NEAL, LEANNE
SAUNDERS, MATT NOONAN, TAIKA WAITITI
BASED ON THE BOOK *WILD PORK AND
WATERCRESS* WRITTEN BY BARRY CRUMP
SCREENPLAY BY TAIKA WAITITI
DIRECTED BY TAIKA WAITITI

For more information about our titles please visit
penguinrandomhouse.co.nz